'I wanted any other for—'

'There isn't,' she snapped. 'Short of offering to marry me yourself.'

Dylan laughed. It was a rich, confident sound. In any other circumstances she would have wanted to join in. 'Perhaps that's exactly what I should do,' he said. 'The only thing that would really make the grade, right?'

'I wasn't serious.'

'I dare you, Annabelle.' There was a light of challenge and determination in his expression that made her uncomfortable. 'I dare you to consider the proposition. Think about it…'

DOCTORS DOWN-UNDER

In Medical Romance™ you'll find a special kind of doctor. Flying doctors, bush doctors, family doctors and city specialists from Sydney, Brisbane or Auckland. Whether they're battling with life and love decisions in the hot and harsh locations of the wilderness or dealing with the personal and medical dramas of city life, they exude a determination, dedication and an earthy charm that only comes from Down-Under.

DOCTORS DOWN-UNDER

They're irresistible

From Mills & Boon® Medical Romance™

Lilian Darcy is Australian, but has strong ties to the USA through her American husband. They have four growing children, and currently live in Canberra, Australia. Lilian has written over forty romance novels, and still has more story ideas crowding into her head than she knows what to do with. Her work has appeared on the Waldenbooks romance bestsellers list, and two of her plays have been nominated for major Australian writing awards. 'I'll keep writing as long as people keep reading my books,' she says. 'It's all I've ever wanted to do, and I love it.'

THE SURGEON'S PROPOSAL

BY

LILIAN DARCY

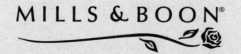

MILLS & BOON®

First published in Great Britain 2003
Harlequin Mills & Boon Limited,
Eton House, 18-24 Paradise Road, Richmond, Surrey TW9 1SR

© Lilian Darcy 2003

ISBN 0 263 83431 X

Set in Times Roman 10 ½ on 12 pt.
03-0303-45307

Printed and bound in Spain
by Litografia Rosés, S.A., Barcelona

CHAPTER ONE

'ARE you on your mobile, Dr Calford?'

'Yes, but don't worry. I've only moved three car lengths in the last ten minutes, so I'm not exactly a danger to other road users.'

'I'm sorry, Dr Calford, I didn't catch that.'

'Never mind, Lesley.' Dylan Calford raised his voice above the background noise of peak-hour traffic. 'There's nothing that can't wait. We'll pick it up next week, OK?'

'Enjoy the wedding,' the orthopaedic clinic secretary carolled cheerfully.

Dylan swallowed the dampening response that sprang to his lips, saying instead, 'And you enjoy your weekend, Lesley.' He knew that, like most working women with a family, she deserved to.

He flipped his phone shut and concentrated on the traffic. Brisbane roads were like tangled spaghetti at the best of times, and five o'clock on a Friday afternoon was not one of those. Being January, it was a *hot* Friday afternoon, too. With the sun pouring through Dylan's front windscreen, the car's air-conditioning couldn't keep up, and he felt sticky all over.

He was already late. Didn't know why he was going to this wedding in the first place. He was cynical about weddings at the moment. He didn't altogether *want* to feel this way, but after the debacle he'd endured with Sarah... There really was something too incongruous about proceeding directly from a meeting with his divorce lawyer to a ceremony designed to shackle two more innocent people together in the dubious bonds of wedlock.

'Like lambs to the slaughter,' he muttered. A crucial three metres of space opened up ahead and he was able to crawl forward far enough to turn left into a quiet side street which *should* cut through in the direction of St Lucia.

Not that Dr Alexander Sturgess remotely resembled a lamb, of course.

Traffic lights ahead. Red, naturally. Dylan had chronic bad luck with traffic. As a result, he'd learned to be alert and super-competent in the way he navigated the sprawling city. That was a plus. All the same, he would have preferred to have been one of those fortunate souls for whom green lights, empty lanes and parking spaces appeared in his path like magic.

The sun was spearing into his eyes, half blinding him and making him sleepy. He and Alex had both been in emergency surgery half the night, putting a nineteen-year-old motorbike rider back together after a horrific crash. Head injury, complicated fractures, internal injuries. It was one of those times when you didn't know whether to even hope that he would live. The metal plates and pins now keeping the young man's bones in place were the least of his problems.

As befitted a senior orthopaedic specialist and a man about to get married, Alex had then taken the rest of the day off. Dylan, in contrast, had tackled his senior's scheduled surgical list, done a three-hour fracture clinic, which had run late, made hospital rounds and met his lawyer. The man was probably on the phone with Sarah's lawyer right now, presenting the details of the proposed settlement he and Dylan had worked out together.

Would it pass muster? Dylan suspected not. Sarah apparently valued the support she'd given him during his past two years of specialist orthopaedic training more highly than he did.

'Thank God we didn't have kids!' he muttered.

Were children on the agenda for Alex and Annabelle? He imagined so. Alex would want to per-petuate the Sturgess dynasty. And Annabelle, aka Theatre Sister Annabelle Drew... Didn't she have a child already? Yes, he was sure she did. Not hers, but one she'd had dumped on her a year or so ago. Her sister's little boy, or something.

Dylan didn't know the exact circumstances. Sister Drew didn't splash her personal life around during surgery like antiseptic solution, the way some people did. She was one of the few women who, in many ways, actually suited the anachronistic title of 'Sister' that was still used for senior nurses in Australian hospitals.

She was composed, contained, warm and highly competent. Polite. Honourable. *Good*. The kind of woman men didn't swear in front of.

Except Alex, Dylan revised. Alex swore during surgery the way he used a scalpel—deliberately, and with precision.

And Annabelle laughs at dirty jokes, he thought. As long as they're actually funny.

She had a lovely laugh. It was gurgly and rich, and came from deep inside her diaphragm.

So perhaps I'm wrong about the swearing thing. Perhaps it's just me who doesn't swear in front of her. That *goodness* thing... I probably don't have the slightest idea about who she really is at all.

The thought discomfited him a little, for some reason. This marriage to Alex, for example. Unlikely, wasn't it, if Annabelle Drew was the woman Dylan believed her to be?

The light turned green and he made a little more progress before getting stopped on a steep hill, which necessitated a noisy handbrake start once the car ahead began to move. Dylan's shirt was glued to his back, and it felt far too limp for a garment he'd only put on an hour ago.

Up ahead. Was that it? At last, yes!

Except that three circuits of the parking area revealed that there were no spaces, which forced Dylan into the next street and delayed his arrival by a further five minutes.

Now I really am in a foul mood! Dylan realised. I wish I'd turned down the invitation.

But his senior colleague would have read more into this than was intended. Alex had a tendency to do that.

Dylan hurried through the entrance of the elegant function centre and asked, 'Sturgess-Drew wedding? I'm late.'

'Straight through.'

'Thanks.'

He opened one half of a double, frosted glass door, slid through the gap, narrowly avoided colliding with a potted palm directly ahead, and discovered that he'd arrived halfway through the ceremony itself. A string quartet waited patiently on a large, draped dais. Guests, seated in neat rows, listened politely as a civil marriage celebrant droned out a syrupy poem.

It was almost impossible to hear. In the front row, a little boy was squirming energetically in the arms of a rather frail-looking woman and yelling, 'No! Don't want to sit down! Don't want to sit down!' He looked to be around two years old.

There were barely any empty seats. Just one, in fact, at the end of the same short row where the little boy was refusing to sit. Dylan edged his way along the side aisle towards it, hoping Alex wouldn't notice his terrible timing.

Again, it was the kind of thing that Dr Alexander Sturgess, MB, BS, M.Sc., FRACS, FA Orth. A., would take personally. Alex never considered that other people might have vindictive ex-wives and verbose divorce lawyers, late-running clinics and bad luck with traffic.

Dylan admired Alex Sturgess as a surgeon, which was why he'd returned to Coronation Hospital to train with him after a couple of rotations in hospitals elsewhere in Queensland. As a man, however, Alex wasn't exactly a role model he strove to emulate.

Easing into the seat, Dylan could hear a little better. The celebrant intoned more flowery words about love. Alex looked as if he'd forgotten to paint an expression on his face—other than, perhaps, a faint mist of approval—and Annabelle looked very, very nervous. The pale grey suit that the groom wore was wrong. Expensive, but wrong. It made Alex's skin tone look washed out, and stressed the fact that his once blond hair was heavily greyed. He was actually a much better looking specimen of manhood than he appeared today.

Oh, shut up! Dylan told himself. Who are you, to

be this critical? Just sit through it, wish them every happiness and let them get on with it!

No.

No.

Annabelle's dress was lovely. She had resisted the current vogue for strapless wedding gowns, in which most brides looked as if they had a single, log-shaped breast plastered across their chest. Dylan suspected, too, that she had an unsuitably freckly back and shoulders. Instead, she wore some draped confection in warm cream silk.

Portrait neckline, was it called? Anyway, it gave her a classic, regal aura and made her curvy figure look perfect. Her shoulder-length dark hair was piled up in glossy curlicues and tendrils. Her brown eyes were huge. Her freckle-dappled skin looked warm and peach perfect. She wasn't beautiful, but she had *something*.

He wasn't wrong about her, Dylan decided. She was going to be miserable with Alex.

The toddler was still struggling and yelling. He was an attractive child, with brown eyes and light brown curly hair, but clearly he wasn't suited to this formal setting. The woman who held him—presumably Annabelle's mother as there was a resemblance—looked grim-faced and at the end of her rope, on the verge of giving up and carrying him out.

Dylan could hear her laboured, wheezy breathing, and remembered overhearing Annabelle talking to another nurse about 'Mum's health'. Emphysema, he thought.

Meanwhile, the little boy was ruining the occasion. Alex clearly thought so. He glared in the child's direction, then frowned tightly. The celebrant reached the meat-and-potatoes part of the ceremony. Traditional and churchy, this bit. Alex's idea? It didn't really fit, after those chintzy poems.

'If anyone here present knows any reason…'

The celebrant raised his voice, struggling to be heard above, 'Put me *down*, Gwanma!'

'May they speak now, or forever hold their peace.'

'Yes, *I* do!' Dylan muttered darkly but very distinctly. 'You're making a terrible mistake!'

They'd heard.

Not the whole congregation, but the ones who counted. Annabelle's mother and Annabelle herself. Alex. The celebrant. The bridesmaid and the best man. The first two rows of guests. Lord, had he said it that loudly?

Apparently.

It didn't help that the little boy had suddenly gone quiet. A plastic lollipop stick protruding from his mouth explained this unlikely development.

Dylan began to sweat. Again.

Alex and Annabelle had both turned in his direction. Alex was looking slack-jawed and appalled, Annabelle startled and bewildered. The bridesmaid was gulping in air, and had a hand pressed to her ribcage. The best man was staring in horror.

Even Annabelle's little boy was watching him, happily sucking on his lollipop, while 'Gwanma' looked as if she had fully expected some kind of ghastly last straw at some point during the afternoon, but hadn't thought it was going to be this.

'I'm sorry,' Dylan barked. Instinctively, he stepped forward. This was another mistake. He was standing just a foot or two from Annabelle now, and right beside her. 'I didn't mean it.' But he *had* meant it. 'It was…' a moment of indulgent madness '…a joke. It was nothing. Please, uh, carry on.'

Alex wasn't buying it. The slack jaw had hardened. The washed-out complexion had refined to white around his nostrils.

'A joke?' His voice rasped. 'That's ridiculous! People don't joke in the middle of a wedding. You have a reputation as a loose cannon in some circles, Dylan, and I've chosen to ignore it, but *this*… What do you mean by it?'

He looked from Dylan to Annabelle and back again, and the action seemed to link the two of them together, standing shoulder to shoulder, as they now were.

'Dylan? Annabelle?' His voice rose.

It was obvious that he suspected an affair. Annabelle had gone bright red. The first two rows of guests were watching in strained silence, like the audience at an amateur play in which the cast have forgotten their lines. Further back, there was whispering, as those who hadn't heard Dylan's words tried to fathom what was going on. On the string quartet's dais, the cellist let her fingers slip and the strings of her instrument squawked.

'Nothing,' Annabelle said. 'Nothing, Alex.' She clasped her hands together. The gesture could have meant either 'Believe me' or 'Forgive me'. Dylan knew it was the former, but Alex clearly wasn't so sure.

Taking another edgy step forward, which brought the billowing skirt of Annabelle's dress washing around his trouser-clad legs, Dylan said, 'Really, Alex, I'm sorry. I know what you're thinking and it's my fault, but, no, it's…' He cleared his throat. 'Nothing like that.'

Annabelle's bridal fragrance enveloped him, evocative and sweet.

'It isn't, Alex. Honestly,' she echoed. Shaking, she laid a hand on her groom's arm. From this perspective, Dylan could see the slope of her right breast where the neckline of her dress gaped a little with her movement. Too many heartbeats passed before he looked away. 'You can't possibly believe—'

'It doesn't matter what I believe,' Alex said. 'It's what other people believe, and it's fairly obvious what they'll believe about this!'

'Garbage!' Dylan put in helpfully.

'Then, please, let's just…get on with it,' Annabelle begged, ignoring him. 'The way you're reacting is only making things worse. People are whispering, and—'

'Oh, it's *my* fault?' Alex's nostrils flared again.

'No, I'm not saying that, but—'

'It's my fault,' Dylan interposed. 'That's clear. Annabelle's right. Please, just get on with it.'

But Alex had a look on his face now. It happened in surgery very occasionally if he was tired and absently asked for the wrong size of clamp or something. Most surgeons would simply correct themselves and go on, but Alex could never do that. He would doggedly proceed with a piece of equipment that was less than ideal, rather than lose face by admitting to a mistake. Fortunately, he was a good enough surgeon to carry it off, but this wasn't surgery, this was his wedding.

For heaven's sake, get over it, Dylan wanted to tell

him. Don't lose your sense of proportion. But he knew it was already too late.

'No, I won't *get on with it*,' Alex said coldly. 'Are you coming, Peter?'

'Yes,' said the best man, who had to be Alex's younger brother. He blinked, like an animal caught in a bright light. 'Yes. Right. Of course.'

Without another word, Alex spun neatly around, strode down the centre aisle and out the glass door through which Dylan had entered just a few minutes earlier. Peter hurried after him. In the dead silence that had now fallen over the assembled guests, just two sounds could be heard—the squeak of the door as it swung closed again, and the lusty sound of one little boy slurping on a red lollipop.

The silence didn't last for long.

In seconds, the sound of voices had swelled from a buzz to a roar. Annabelle's silk skirt swished against Dylan's legs again as she whirled to face him. She was furious.

'Why did you do it? A joke? You can't think I'll swallow that! It was malicious! You know Alex as well as I do, Dylan Calford. You must have known he'd take it as a personal insult or worse. *Why* did you do it!'

In hundreds of hours of working together during surgery, Dylan had never seen her brown eyes blaze that way before. Her chest was heaving. The dress had slipped a little, and one creamy shoulder was bared. Her cheeks were still fiery red. She looked electric and wild and more stunningly attractive than he'd ever have thought she could...but, then, he'd never seen her dressed for her own wedding before. A dangerous new awareness stirred inside him.

'Why?' he echoed. 'Why?'

As fast as a computer scanning its hard drive, he ran through all the possible placatory falsehoods at his disposal and rejected every one of them. He was left, therefore, with the bald truth, so he said that, aware even as he spoke the words of how inadequate they sounded.

'Because I knew you wouldn't be happy.'

Annabelle was not grateful for the insight.

In a low voice, she said, 'I wanted this marriage. I needed it. I was going to give up work and take Duncan out of child-care. He hates it, and it's not good for him. I was going to spend more time with my mother, who isn't well, who isn't going to get better, and who needs me, too.'

'Is that what marriage is—?'

She rode right over the top of him. 'I was going to relax, for once, with a man I respected and cared for—*care* for—at my side, a man who's made it clear that I'm important to him, and that we can create a good partnership together. I had faith in that partnership! How dare you impose your own shallow definition of marital happiness? And how dare you presume to make that sort of judgement about us?'

'Not Alex,' Dylan corrected. 'Just you.'

'How dare you imagine you know me that well? No wonder Alex thought we were having an affair!'

The bridesmaid squeaked and covered her mouth with her hands.

'Darling…' came a shaky, smoke-damaged voice.

Annabelle turned. 'Yes, Mum?'

'Can you take Duncan now? He won't go to anyone else, and I just…can't. I need my oxygen from the car, and my inhaler. I shouldn't have thought I could get by for so long without them.'

'Oh, Lord, Mum, I'm sorry!' Annabelle muttered. She blinked several times, and Dylan realised it was because she was fighting tears. She reached out for the little boy, but he'd had enough, lollipop notwithstanding, and wriggled immediately to the ground.

'Splore!' he said.

'No, we can't explore now, love.' She bent to him, and Dylan got a serious and spectacular view of her breasts, as smooth as ivory and as plump as fresh-baked rolls. His groin tightened unexpectedly, and he felt as if someone had barged into him and knocked him sideways. Now was not the moment to have this happen.

'Want to explore with me, Dunc?' the bridesmaid offered tentatively, just behind Annabelle.

Too late. Duncan was already off and away, through the crowds of guests, who were milling uneasily in aisles and between rows of seats. The bridesmaid followed him, way too slowly. Dylan was still rooted to the spot. For several reasons. Annabelle straightened, and a sigh escaped between her teeth.

'He'll come back, won't he?' Annabelle's mother said.

'If he doesn't head straight for the street and get mown down by a car, the little monkey-love.'

'I meant Alex.'

'Oh.' Annabelle sighed again. 'No, Mum, I don't think he will. Alex is…not the type who cools off quickly.'

'But surely he'll realise—'

'I'd better go after Duncan, Mum. Linda's had no experience with kids. I'll bring your oxygen and your inhaler, and I'll tell everyone that they're welcome to stay. You can pass the word around, too. Get the music playing, perhaps? There's no sense all this food and planning going to waste. And then I'd better phone and cancel our hotel…'

Gathering up the folds of her dress, she smiled distractedly at several guests and began to make her way down the aisle. Following her, Dylan spotted Duncan at the back of the string quartet's dais, and pointed him out to Annabelle.

Again, she wasn't grateful.

'*You* won't be staying to eat, I don't suppose,' she said. It was an order rather than a question, and her chin was raised. 'But perhaps you'd care to mention, on your way out, that cocktails and dinner are still on for those who want them?'

'Sure. Of course,' he agreed, knowing how completely inadequate it was.

He did as she'd asked, heading gradually towards the beckoning glass doors. After fielding several questions along the lines of 'What on earth did you say?' and 'Oh, was it *you*, then?' he was finally able to make his escape. He'd never been so relieved in his life.

At home, once he'd peeled off his limp clothing and had a cold shower, a message on his answering-machine awaited him.

It was from Sarah.

'I've heard your offer, and it's insulting. We're preparing a counter-offer over the weekend, and your lawyer will hear from mine on Monday.'

Am I that out of touch with reality? Dylan wondered, after he'd erased the message. We were only married for two years. I was working. She was working. We employed a cleaner. We ate take-away meals, or I cooked. We kept separate bank accounts, and split the mortgage payments. For six months of that time, I was on rotation in Townsville and we only saw each other every second weekend.

In fact, they'd been far too scrupulous about maintaining a degree of separation in their lives, he now considered. Sarah hadn't wanted to come to Townsville. Perhaps their marriage would have lasted longer, and been happier, if they'd joined themselves to each other more completely. And perhaps he would then have felt that Sarah was entitled to the top-heavy percentage of their assets that she was obviously planning to claim.

Still stewing over it, and over the wedding fiasco, he made himself some salad and one of those nutritionally challenged instant dried pasta meals that people took on camping trips. Then he bored himself with television for several hours and dropped into bed at eleven, seeking oblivion.

It didn't come. He felt like a heel and resolved to himself, I'll make it up to Annabelle. That's the least I can do.

Go and see Alex, try and explain. Cover the cost of the reception. Ring each and every guest personally. Anything. Whatever Annabelle wanted.

Had this whole mess happened because of the divorce, or because he was a really terrible person? Until things had gone pear-shaped with Sarah, he'd have said his life was in an impeccable state. Priorities in order. Heart in the right place. Career on track. Judgement damn near flawless.

Hang on, though! Had he lost that much faith in himself? Rebellion began to stir inside him.

Annabelle Drew, I saved your backside this afternoon, no matter how you twist your definition of marital happiness.

Poking at his feelings a little more, he discovered, to his surprise, that he was angry with her. Disappointed, too. Somehow, she was a woman of whom he would have expected better. Better priorities. Better principles. Better sense.

I *will* make it up to her, if she'll let me. But she's wrong to blame me for this!

Rolling onto his stomach in a twisted sheet, Dylan slept at last.

'Thank heavens that's over!' Helen Drew said to her daughter, as the final straggle of wedding guests headed for their cars, later than both of them had hoped. She had her portable oxygen close beside her, and really should have been using it more tonight. Her breathing sounded terrible, despite the use of her inhaler, and she looked even worse. 'You did a fabulous job, darling. I was proud of you.'

Annabelle felt her mother's arms wrap around her like a comfortable quilt. On the dais vacated by the departing string quartet, Duncan had fallen asleep at last, about fifteen minutes ago. And Linda had gone, too, thank goodness. She was a good and loyal friend, great at helping Annabelle with tax and finance questions, but was useless, and knew it, with kids, the elderly and sick people. Her ineffectual offers of help had, in the end, been something of a strain.

'You mean the fact that my face felt as if it was about to drop off didn't show from the outside?' Annabelle said to her mother.

'Well, of course it did, but people expected that.

They knew you were upset.' Annabelle's mother hesitated for a moment. 'Life will go on, you know.'

'Oh, I know that, Mum.' Although she couldn't quite imagine it at the moment.

She felt like one of those cartoon characters who stepped off a cliff, but didn't start falling until the gravity of their situation hit home. Her mind ticked and rattled like an engine out of tune.

Cancel the hotel for this weekend. Cancel the two-week honeymoon, planned for just over a month from now, at a time when Alex had been able to make some space in his schedule. Thank goodness she hadn't handed in her notice at the hospital yet! Where was Alex right now? At home?

'And anyway, you and Alex, I'm sure, will patch things up,' Helen said. 'It would seem silly not to get married just because some idiot of a man decided to get clever during the ceremony.'

Which of those misconceptions, if any, to tackle first? Annabelle wondered.

First misconception—she and Alex weren't going to patch things up. She knew that. Their relationship was over.

He had put so much thought and time and money into making theirs a perfect, elegant wedding, befitting the strong and sensible partnership they had hoped to create together. He'd wanted a ceremony and reception that would set a benchmark for friends and colleagues to aspire to, the sort of occasion that people would talk about for years. Well, they'd achieved the latter goal! Unfortunately, not in the way he'd wanted.

And he was a very stubborn man. Slinking off next week to a sparse little ceremony in a bureaucrat's office wouldn't make the grade, even leaving out the question of Alex's loss of face.

Which Alex would never leave out. And he was probably right—people would gossip.

Second misconception—Dylan Calford wasn't an idiot.

She'd known him, on and off, for three and a half years now. In some ways, she knew him better than she knew Alex, since there wasn't such a gap in status between them. She knew what he looked like first thing in the morning, fresh from a snatched sleep in the doctors' on-call room. She knew what he ate for lunch, and the places he'd been to for holidays since his marriage. They called each other by their first names.

He was proving himself as a fine surgeon, he was good to work with, and by all scales of character measurement, he was a pretty decent man. What Annabelle knew of him, she liked—*had* liked until today—and along with the rest of the hospital staff who worked with him, she felt for him over the issue of his divorce. He wasn't quite the same person he'd been a couple of years ago. Harder. More cynical, and less patient.

And, finally, he hadn't 'decided to get clever'. He hadn't intended his words to be overheard. Possibly, he hadn't intended to speak them out loud at all.

Which means he genuinely thinks our marriage would have been a mistake.

How could something be a mistake when you needed it so badly? Annabelle knew that she and Alex weren't in love the way most couples believed themselves to be when they married. They'd talked about that, seriously and at length.

Alex had exhibited his worst qualities today—as he sometimes did in surgery—but in their private time, he was thoughtful and interesting. They respected each other. He approved of her. They could talk about plans without friction. He was a tender, undemanding lover, and he worked hard at his relationship with Duncan.

And, oh, dear Lord, she'd *needed* their marriage! She *needed* to be able to give up work for a few years in order to focus her attention on caring for her mother and Duncan. She *needed* Alex's financial support, not for herself but for the people she loved.

When they'd started going out together four months ago, it had been like being rescued from a dragon's lair by a white knight. She'd started sleeping again. She'd seen light at the end of the tunnel.

Whereas now…

Suddenly, she felt sick. Anger towards Dylan Calford rose in her throat like bile. The concern he evidently had about the dire possibility of her making a mistake in marriage, of her 'being unhappy', was a luxury she couldn't afford.

'I wouldn't have *let* it be a mistake!' she muttered to herself. 'I would have made it work, no matter what it took. I would have been happy! Imposing his cynical stance on other people just because he's having a bad divorce is unforgivably arrogant!'

'Are you angry with him?' her mother asked.

'Yes. Absolutely and utterly furious!' Annabelle said aloud.

'Don't let it get in the way when you talk.' Mum put out her hand and rested it heavily on Annabelle's arm. 'And try to talk to him soon. He acted out of pride. He'll make it up to you. I'm *sure* you can work it out.'

'Oh, Mum, no, I'm not angry with Alex. I understand why he walked out. It's Dylan Calford I'll never forgive for all this!' Annabelle said.

CHAPTER TWO

DYLAN appeared at Annabelle's house at nine-thirty the next morning.

Duncan had awoken, as usual, at six. No matter how late he stayed up, he never slept in. Right now, he was running wildly around the back garden, pushing a big toy truck, and he would barely slacken his pace all day. Annabelle often wondered what sort of a child his father had been. This active? This unstoppable? There was no one to ask about him.

'Hello,' she said coolly to Alex's registrar at the front door of her little weatherboard Queenslander.

'Uh, yeah, hi…' he answered.

'I suppose you want to come in,' Annabelle prompted him, not sure why she was taking the trouble to help him out, even to this limited extent.

She had never seen him so at a loss for words. Had never seen him dressed so casually either. His body was one hundred per cent male. Broad shoulders, strong legs, dark hair and darker eyes, football player's waist and hips. Orthopaedic surgeons had to be strong.

Since this was Brisbane in January, he wore shorts—navy blue and topped with a polo shirt subtly patterned in a beige and khaki print. He was freshly showered and shaven, and radiated an energy that was only partly physical.

He looked good, and he'd recovered his equilibrium already. He was intimidating, if she'd been in the mood to feel intimidated by anyone. Right now, she wasn't.

'Look, I won't apologise again,' he said, his tone that of a man who was sure of his ground.

'No, don't,' she agreed. 'But, please, don't stay here on the veranda. It's cooler out the back, and I need to keep an eye on Duncan.'

'Sure.' The word sharpened his slight American accent. Annabelle knew he had been here since his early teens, had been a star rugby player at Brisbane's most illustrious boys' school and held Australian citizenship, but sometimes his Chicago origins still showed.

She led the way through the house and he spoke behind her. 'But I do want to do what I can to make this whole thing less difficult for you.'

'Sure.' She turned her head and smiled as she echoed the word he'd used, but the smile didn't do much to soak up the pool of dripping sarcasm in her tone. There was nothing he could do to make this 'less difficult'!

He didn't reply, yet somehow this time his silence was much stronger than some bleating protest would have been. Her spine prickled suddenly.

They reached the back veranda, which was shaded by the riot of tropical growth that threatened to encroach upon it. Along the paved path, Duncan was still making truck sounds, while the small and securely fenced swimming pool beckoned invitingly in a patch of sunshine. Hibiscus and frangipani gave bright and sweetly scented accents of colour, and the wooden floor of the veranda was cool and smooth under Annabelle's bare feet.

From somewhere, as she invited Dylan to sit in one of the cane-backed chairs, came the thought, At least now I don't have to move. To Alex's large, air-conditioned and professionally decorated river-front house. They'd been planning to sell this place, or rent it out as an investment.

'You have a nice little place,' Dylan observed.

'I'm fond of it,' she agreed.

That was an understatement. She loved this small eighty-year-old cottage, perched on an absurd patch of land that had a cliff for a front garden and a crooked walkway of twenty-seven steps up from the street to the front door. This was one of the older areas of Brisbane, just a few kilometres from the city centre.

She didn't mention to Dylan that the mortgage on the house was stretching her finances far too thinly, now that she had child-care fees for Duncan on top of it.

Change to night shifts if I can. Mum's health is only going to get worse, but hopefully she'll have a few good years yet, and by then Duncan will be at school. As for the money...

The repetitious thoughts droned on in her head. Cutting them off, she offered, 'Would you like tea or coffee? Or something cool?'

'Coffee would be great.' The cane chair creaked a little as he shifted his weight.

'Can you keep an eye on Duncan for me while I get it?'

'Of course.'

Mad. She had been stark, raving mad to invite him in, Annabelle decided in the kitchen. He didn't particularly deserve a fair hearing, she considered, so why give him one?

Habit.

This was how she'd first become involved with Alex. He had been particularly brutal during surgery one day several months ago. Had had her on the verge of tears, which not many surgeons could have done. And he'd invited her out to dinner as an apology. 'And to prove to you that what you see in surgery is only a small part of who I am. I should probably invite the entire theatre staff in rotation!'

Although it had seemed a little out of character, she had taken the invitation at face value, and had been surprised at the ultra-expensive restaurant he'd chosen. She had been even more surprised when he'd kissed her at the end of the evening. She hadn't picked up on his intention until it had happened.

It probably hadn't been until their fourth or fifth date that she'd gone beyond the fair hearing thing and had really started to appreciate Alex for who he was. His clever mind, his knowledge of wine and food, his informed opinions and the fact that he'd made his approval of her very clear.

It had been like an audition, or a job interview. She'd realised that. He'd been making sure she was suitable. He had been impressed to discover that her mother was *that* Helen Drew, the widow of Sir William Drew, QC, and when he'd then heard from Annabelle that her father's finances had been in a disastrous state on his death several years ago, it hadn't put him off.

At the same time, Annabelle had been assessing Alex in a similar way. For a start, they'd got on well. Always had something to talk about. Never yelled at each other, if you didn't count surgery. Annabelle didn't like the way Alex behaved in surgery, but he defended himself.

'Sorry. It's bloody hard. I'm a prima donna, I know. But there's too much at stake, Annabelle, during a difficult operation. I'm going to swear if something goes wrong, and I'm going to yell at whoever's responsible. That, by the way, is never me! Don't try and get me to change.'

OK. Fair enough. She could tolerate it.

More importantly, from her point of view, Alex realised that Duncan was a permanent fixture in her life, and always took him into consideration. He was happy about supporting both of them, and understood that her mother required a huge amount of Annabelle's time and care as well. He actively preferred that she give up work.

'If you never go back at all, that's fine with me.'

This wasn't quite how she felt. She loved her career but, even leaving aside Mum's needs, Duncan just wasn't the kind of child that did well in the structured environment of a child-care centre, and she couldn't ignore that. She had begun to see unpleasant shifts in his developing personality that upset her deeply, and she knew that the overworked and underpaid child-care centre staff breathed sighs of relief when he went home each day.

Duncan had been carelessly conceived during a holiday fling with a Greek barman, carelessly brought into the world and casually abandoned by his mother, Annabelle's sister Victoria. Vic hadn't intended to abandon him permanently, of course. She'd simply left him in Annabelle's care when he was ten months old, while she went on an adventure holiday in Borneo.

'Eleven days. You don't mind, do you, Belle?'

No, she didn't mind. She loved her baby nephew, and she had days off work owing to her.

Six days into the trip, Victoria had been killed in a landslide on the side of a jungle-clad mountain. It was an exotic end to an exotic life, and a difficult start for a little boy. He deserved better, and he was going to get it in future, Annabelle had vowed.

Only now, because of Dylan Calford, he wasn't.

The electric jug boiled and she poured steaming water onto the little mounds of shiny granules at the bottom of each mug, creating a hissing sound. The coffee smelled good and rich and fresh, but unmistakably like instant. She had real ground beans, and a whiz-bang Christmas-gift coffee-machine, but wasn't going to waste either the coffee or the machine on Dylan Calford today. The coffee took longer to make that way, and might give him the mistaken impression that she wasn't furious.

'Here.'

She handed him the muddy black brew, and plonked a plate of sweet biscuits onto the coffee-table. There wasn't much room on it at the moment. Duncan was running back and forth between his toy chest and the table, depositing his trucks and cars there one by one in a long, snaking row. His sound effects were loud.

'Active little boy,' Dylan commented.

'He doesn't have ADHD,' Annabelle said.

'Did I say—?'

'A lot of people have said it. The manager of his child-care centre wanted him assessed.'

'But you didn't think it was necessary?'

'No. Because when he's with me, he's fine. Active, yes. Top-of-the-chart active, but I read up on the sub-

ject when the issue was first raised, and he doesn't
show any of the other signs of attention deficit hy-
peractivity disorder. The psychologist I finally took
him to agreed. His concentration is fully engaged
when he's interested in something. He's not aggres-
sive, unless he's handled aggressively first.' Or not
often, anyway, she revised inwardly, thinking of a
couple of recent incidents at child-care. These were
the reason she'd consulted the child psychologist, and
she'd found his ideas on the issue very sensible. She
summarised them briefly to Dylan.

'He can't express his feelings very well yet. His
language skills aren't good enough. So he gets frus-
trated in a situation where he's not happy, and there
have been a couple of incidents of biting and kicking
at his child-care centre. A lot of young children go
through a similar stage, and they grow out of it, if it's
handled in the right way.'

If. A big 'if', in this case, when Annabelle herself
couldn't be with him, and the staff at child-care didn't
have the resources to give him the extra attention he
needed.

Knowing she could talk for minutes on end about
Duncan, his difficulties and her feelings, she finished,
'He just likes to be on the go, to head for the horizon
and explore.'

Like Vic had. Perhaps he had received his temper-
ament from her.

'Parents usually know best,' Dylan said.

'I *am* his parent!' She glared at him. 'Or the closest
thing he's got to one, anyhow.'

'Yes, that's what I meant. You'd know, and I'm
guessing you're not influenced too much by wishful
thinking either. Or not usually.'

He frowned, and Annabelle flushed. Was that a reference to Alex and their marriage plans? It was! She'd blurted out far too much to Dylan yesterday in her anger.

'Why are you here, Dylan?' she asked him coldly.

'To make an offer. Some kind of compensation. I want to cover the cost of the reception at least.'

'Alex is the one to approach about that, although I doubt he'd accept it. *I* wouldn't!'

'And ask you if there's any other way I can make up for—'

'There isn't,' she snapped. 'Short of offering to marry me yourself.'

It had to be one of the most ill-thought-out suggestions she'd ever made, a product of fatigue and stress, and disappointment and anger, and something else she didn't have a name for. Something new. She didn't usually come out with wild statements like that.

Dylan laughed. It was a rich, confident sound. In any other circumstances, she would have wanted to join in. 'Perhaps that's exactly what I should do,' he said. 'The only thing that would really make the grade, right?'

'I didn't mean—'

'Thanks. You've made me feel better.' He was still grinning at her, his dark gaze sweeping over her like a caress. It disturbed her.

'How?'

'By proving to me that I did the right thing. The insane thing, under the circumstances, and I hadn't realised it would be the show-stopping announcement that it was, but if you could propose me as a substitute husband—'

'I wasn't serious.'

'One day later.'

'I wasn't serious!'

'Even as a joke, then doesn't that tell you—?'

'Nothing.' She shook her head sharply, clenched teeth aching. 'It was a stupid, meaningless thing to say. It doesn't tell me anything.'

'I dare you, Annabelle.' There was a light of challenge and determination in his expression now that made her uncomfortable. He was leaning forward in his seat, his strength casually apparent. 'I dare you to consider the proposition. I've got just as much to offer you as Alex does. Not exactly the same things, perhaps, but equivalent. Better, possibly, in some areas. Think about it.'

And suddenly, graphically, she was.

She was thinking about a wedding—symbol of solved problems—and a wedding night, and a bed with Dylan Calford in it. Naked. Or possibly not quite naked yet, but with some snug-fitting black stretch fabric across his groin. And smiling. The way he was smiling now, with a challenge glinting in his eyes, and a wicked, delicious expression that said, I can read your mind.

She went hot all over. My sainted aunt! She'd never thought of Dylan Calford that way before! He'd been engaged or married or absorbed in his divorce for the entire three and a half years she'd known him, and that had meant he'd been off limits. Not just in her eyes, but in his own.

He didn't give off the knowing, overtly sexual vibe that available, good-looking men so often exuded. And, anyway, they rarely encountered each other outside the demanding environment of surgery, and never away from the hospital. When they worked together, there was always too much else to think about.

Today was different. There were no patients, no colleagues. His property settlement was at the negotiation stage, with the one-year anniversary of his separation already past. The vibe was there, singing and throbbing like the strings of an instrument. Two contradictory feelings warred inside her.

The first was instinct more than thought, and insisted, You'll learn more from this than you ever learned from Alex. The second was an impatient need to reject the whole thing as dangerous, untrustworthy and insignificant.

The second feeling won.

'You don't mean it,' she told Dylan flatly.

Hardly aware of what she was doing, she wrapped her arms across her body to try and stroke away the goose-bumps that had risen on her arms. Her nipples ached, and deep inside her there was a heaviness and a heat that hadn't been there a few minutes ago. Definitely, she didn't want any of it. Not now.

'No,' he agreed. 'You're right. I don't. But you thought about it, didn't you?' His eyes were still fixed on her face.

'Not in the way you mean.'

Or, possibly, *exactly* in the way he'd meant.

Had he been aware of the vibe he'd given off? The potency of it? The delicious wickedness of it? The fact that she'd absorbed it, wrapped herself in it and reflected it right back at him? Or was he giving it off unconsciously?

'Well, think about it some more,' he said. Or, rather, *ordered*.

He took what had to be a scorching gulp of his

coffee, without apparently noticing the heat. If he had a tendency not to notice heat, that was good, a relief…and a reprieve.

'There's no need to think about it any more,' she said sharply. 'Not for a second.'

'I wonder.'

Meanwhile, Duncan had become bored with the car and truck game, and every vehicle he owned was now lined up on the coffee-table like a peak-hour traffic jam. 'Go inna pool, Mummy?' he said hopefully.

'In a little while, love,' she answered.

A swim would be great. Bruising, with the way Duncan liked to hurl himself off the edge and into her arms in the water. His eager little legs always collided painfully with her thighs as he held her tight and instinctively kicked like a frog beneath the water. But it would cool her down. The building heat in the air was extra sticky today.

Duncan had already run off in search of towels. He'd probably come back with six of them.

As soon as he had gone, Dylan asked curiously, 'He calls you that? Mummy?'

Annabelle went on the defensive at once. 'Mum and I talked about it. We agreed it would be best at this stage. He has no memory of Vic—my sister. We haven't decided when we'll tell him.'

'Tell me how it happened,' he invited quietly. 'Do you mind?'

She stifled a sigh. Sometimes she *did* mind, especially when the questions were nosy, tactless or judgmental. But somehow Dylan Calford seemed to be in her life now, since yesterday. Arrogant in his presumptions, dictatorial in his advice. She was still angry about it, yet at the same time felt her usual over-developed need to be *fair*. Beyond the arrogance, his desire to make amends as far as possible was apparently genuine.

Not that he *can* make amends, she considered inwardly. Is it the thought that counts? Aloud, she said, 'No, I don't mind. She'd gone trekking, and there was an accident. In Borneo. It was in the news. You might have read about it.'

He thought for a moment, then nodded. 'Mmm, yes, I remember now. I'm sorry, I didn't realise that was your sister.'

'I didn't want to talk about it much at work.'

'It must have been hard. For you and your mother.' They weren't flowery words, but she appreciated the depth of sincerity behind them.

'Still can't believe it sometimes,' she admitted. 'Sometimes I—' She broke off and shook her head.

Sometimes she'd hear a voice in a crowded shopping mall and instinctively turn her head because it sounded like Vic. Sometimes, with news or a funny anecdote to tell, she'd pick up the telephone and stop with her finger poised over the first digit of Vic's old phone number, her whole body frozen and a stabbing pain in her stomach.

But she didn't want to tell Dylan Calford about any of that. He didn't prompt her to finish, and she felt a small stirring of gratitude for the fact.

'And there was no father around?' he asked after a moment.

'Not one that we could trace. Vic never even told Mum and me his last name. He didn't know about Duncan and wouldn't have cared, Vic said. It was a holiday romance. She travelled a lot.'

'The adventurous type. Like her son.'

'I'm starting to see that, yes, although at the end of a long day, I always blame his father for the high energy levels!'

'How do you deal with it? How do you know that your full-time care will be better than a child-care centre?' Evidently he remembered exactly what she'd said to him yesterday.

'Because I love him. I…' she searched for the right word '…*champion* him, in a way those very nice girls—really, they're very nice—at child-care just don't have time for, with their ratio of one adult to five kids.'

'That high?'

'It's standard,' she answered. 'I believe in him, and know him well enough to bring out the best in him. I understand what he's trying to tell me, which some people don't. His speech isn't very clear yet, and that frustrates him. I have the time and care to head off his difficult behaviour, and I know when he's overdosed on other kids and needs some time to himself. We go to the park for hours, and just run each other down as if we were two little toys in one of those battery commercials on television. He sleeps well, if an hour or two less than most kids his age. And I'm pretty fit, as a result!'

'Hmm,' Dylan said. There was a pause. 'And what will happen now?'

'He'll stay in child-care. Unless I can juggle my shifts at the hospital, which, of course, I'll try to do.'

Which doesn't deal with the mortgage. There must be some other areas where I can save. If I get an increase on my credit-card limit…

'There's no other choice? Your mother—'

'Has emphysema, as you may have realised. She's

tired and breathless, gets asthma attacks quite often, and can't do much for herself. She could sell her little unit and come and live here, yes, but she's too ill to help with Duncan, other than overnight babysitting, and really too ill to live under the same roof as such an active little boy.'

'Yes, I can understand that.'

'She loves him, but she wouldn't be happy here. Can you stop asking these questions, Dylan? Marrying Alex wasn't just about solving my current family problems. There was a lot more. You mean well. I can see that. But you're trivialising my life, and my choices. It's not helping. Don't try and help, please.'

She lifted her chin and met his gaze steadily, still far more conscious of their two bodies than she wanted to be. What was he thinking? She couldn't tell. His dark eyes were clouded and thoughtful, and he was frowning.

At that moment, Duncan ran back out to the veranda, as expected, with his arms full of towels. One dangling end was dangerously close to tripping up his eager little feet. Turning away from Dylan, Annabelle took the bundle from Duncan quickly, and asked, 'What about your cozzie? Know where that is?'

'Onna line,' he said confidently, and rushed off again, to the far corner of the crowded garden where the rotary clothesline stood, hung with pegged-up garments.

'I should go,' Dylan said, and Annabelle didn't argue. 'Please, think a little more about what I said.'

She laughed. 'The marriage proposal? You didn't mean it. I'm not going to think about it for a second.'

'You're right. I didn't mean it. But think about it

anyway.' His dark gaze collided with hers again. It seemed to trap her, making her hot.

'That doesn't make sense,' she told him.

'Probably not,' he agreed. 'Although I wonder... Maybe one day we'll both understand what it meant.'

Then he shrugged, smiled and stood up, looking long and strong and sturdy. Not at all the kind of man who should make whimsical marriage proposals that he admitted he didn't mean but still wanted her to take seriously.

'Enjoy the pool,' he said, and touched her bare shoulder.

His hand left a warm imprint there, and was gone again in a second. Annabelle's awareness of his touch was unsettling and unwanted. She took him quickly back through the house, and they got through a few last polite phrases, then she closed the door behind him and listened with relief to the confident sound of his feet as he loped down the twenty-seven steps.

She spent a shrieking half-hour in the pool with Duncan, got him dried and dressed and settled him with a video.

Then she phoned Alex.

'I was wondering when you'd call,' he said stiffly.

'It's just on eleven. I wasn't sure whether to...' She trailed off, feeling the phone line between them heavy with stony silence. She tried again, newly determined that there had to be a way to get through this. It was ridiculous to call off a marriage *permanently* because of one meaningless intrusion during the ceremony. They were both mature adults. Alex was almost forty, and she was thirty-two. 'I really wanted to talk, Alex, but I thought we both needed to cool down after last night. I'm just as angry with Dylan as you are.'

Silence.

'And if you still think I gave him any cause to make that idiotic objection, then I'm not sure what to do next, because I *didn't*, and I've told you that, and *he's* told you that…' She paused expectantly.

Silence.

'Which makes me start to wonder if you were just looking for an excuse.'

'Don't be so ridiculous.'

'So we'll get married. A small, discreet ceremony, with—'

'That's impossible. I'm not going to rehash it again.'

'Tell me what you're *feeling*, Alex!' she begged him desperately. 'Just blustering like this, stonewalling anything I say, it's not telling me anything.'

Silence.

'Shall I come over to your place, or do you want to come here?' she suggested.

Silence.

'Dylan wants to pay for the reception. I told him to talk to you about it.'

'So you've seen him? When have you seen him?'

'He came round just now. He obviously feels bad.'

'I can't believe you're defending him, and that you talked to him before you talked to me.'

'I'm not defending him.' *Am I?* 'I'm just letting you know that he'll probably phone you, too. I don't know why he came to me first.'

Silence.

'So, should we talk about—?'

'There's absolutely nothing to talk about at all,' Alex snapped. 'It's out of the question to have him pay for the reception.'

'Well, yes, that's what I thought, but since it was your money, I didn't want to—'

'And it's out of the question to talk about scheduling another ceremony. I won't get over this in a hurry, Annabelle. You're the last person I would have thought the type to trail chaos and melodrama in your wake, but now I'm wondering how many other ex-boyfriends—'

'Dylan Calford isn't an—'

'Or *would-be* boyfriends I can expect to crawl out of the woodwork. I was embarrassed to the core last night. People, no doubt, are already talking and making conjectures. And I don't even think I could look at you at the moment, Annabelle.'

The reproachful crash of the slamming phone invaded Annabelle's left ear, and stinging tears flooded her vision. Today, this hurt in a way it hadn't hurt last night. Last night she'd been angry, and in shock. Now came the full realisation that Alex had dropped her like a hot coal, as if she were tainted in some way.

He'd almost said as much. He'd called her a 'type'. Not the type to attract scandal. Not the type to compromise his reputation and his ambitions. Political ambitions. She knew he had them. President of the Australian Medical Association. Queensland State Minister for Health. But she'd believed herself to mean much more to Alex than a suitably well-bred and stain-resistant political wife, just as he meant more to her than a way out of her family problems.

Annabelle stuffed her knuckles into her mouth and sobbed wildly, until she remembered Duncan in the next room. He would be worried and confused if he saw her like this—red-eyed, swollen-nosed. He had a caring little heart, when he stood still long enough for it to show.

She heard the clatter of his feet as he bounced off the couch to come looking for her, and quickly turned to the kitchen sink to wash away the worst of the mess her face was in. By the time he appeared, she was wearing a smile.

CHAPTER THREE

ANNABELLE and Duncan reached Gumnut Playcare just as it opened, at six-thirty on Monday morning. Annabelle was rostered in Theatre with a seven o'clock start, and timing, as usual, was tight.

'Got your backpack?' she prompted Duncan, then watched as he dragged it slowly across the back seat of the car.

His little face looked sullen and closed and not at all cute.

She helped him put the backpack on, then took his hand and tried to lead him up the path to the front door, but he stalled, pulled out of her grasp and ran off to examine some interesting leaves on a nearby bush.

'We can't look at those now, love,' she told him brightly, but he ignored her. 'I'll be late,' she finished, knowing the concept—and the consequences—were meaningless to a little boy.

Since it was all too likely that either Alex or Dylan, or both of them, would be operating in Theatre Three today, she was doubly anxious to arrive on time.

''Eaves,' Duncan said. His tone was stubborn.

'I know, they're lovely leaves, but we just can't look at them now. This afternoon, OK?'

She hoped, guiltily, that he'd forget. It would be six or later before she got back here, as Mum had a doctor's appointment. Annabelle had cleaned and done laundry for her yesterday, but today, in addition, they would need to stop at the shops on the way back from the doctor. If the doctor was running late, or if she herself was late off work…

A twelve-hour day was too long for a two-year-old.

''Eaves,' he said again.

'Not now, sweetie.'

She picked him up and carried him inside, ignoring the way he wriggled and kicked. He'd been a darling all weekend, sitting rapt and attentive on the couch yesterday afternoon while Mum read to him, 'helping' to hang out the laundry. Today, she already knew he was going to be a demon.

Inside the child-care centre, once she had put him down, he streaked off and began running noisily around the room, without responding to the overly cheerful greetings of Lauren and Carly, the two staff on duty. Annabelle signed him in, unsurprised to find that he was the first name on today's page.

Just then a second child arrived—a four-year-old girl named Katie, prettily dressed and obediently holding her mother's hand. As soon as she saw Duncan, she said in a loud voice, 'That's the naughty boy who bit me, Mummy.'

Annnabelle's stomach flipped. She turned to Lauren. 'You didn't tell me…'

'There's a note in his pocket.' Lauren gestured towards the bright row of cloth 'pockets' running along the wall, where children's artwork and notes for parents were placed. Duncan's was brimming with untidily folded paintings, and Annabelle thought guiltily, When did I last remember to check it? Wednesday?

When she picked him up, she was always so keen to get out of here quickly.

'I'm sorry,' she said. 'I'll speak to him about it.'

Which would be pointless with a two-year-old, when the incident had occurred several days earlier. Katie's mother was glaring at Annabelle, however, and she felt obliged to act tough. Inside, she was crumbling.

'And it's not the first time either, I've heard,' the mother said coldly.

She was right. It wasn't.

But it only ever happened at child-care.

'Can I make an appointment to talk to you?' Annabelle asked Lauren desperately.

'This afternoon?'

'I can't today. I have other commitments.' And tomorrow wasn't any better. 'I'll have to look at my diary. Duncan, Mummy has to go, OK?'

She had to say it twice to get his attention, but when she did, he rushed over and flung his arms around her legs.

'No!'

'You have a great day, OK?'

'No. Don't go.'

'I'll see you later.' Aeons later. 'And we'll have spaghetti for dinner.'

Duncan burst into tears and clung to her legs as she dragged herself towards the door. Lauren intervened, picking him up and talking brightly about blocks and puzzles. He began to kick and struggle, and the brightness was more forced. 'We don't kick, Duncan,' she said.

The little girl's mother walked past, in the wake of a sweet-voiced and perfectly contented, 'I love you, Mummy!'

'I love you too, Katie, my sweetheart angel,' she called back. Smugly, it seemed to Annabelle.

'Just go, Annabelle. He'll be fine in two seconds,' Lauren said.

They both knew it wasn't true.

'Thanks,' Annabelle answered.

Unlocking her car, she heard the little girl's mother muttering pointedly about discipline and aggression and behaviour problems. She was still shaking and queasy as she drove out of the parking area and into the street.

The whole of today's list in Theatre Three consisted of hips and knees, Annabelle discovered when she arrived at Coronation Hospital. Dr Shartles had two hip replacements, then Alex took over for two quite complex knee operations and another hip procedure sandwiched in between, with Dylan assisting. All three were private patients, which meant that Alex would involve himself more thoroughly than he did with public patients having the same surgery.

Dr Shartles's hip replacements went without a hitch, which served as a necessary settling to Annabelle's focus. She enjoyed this aspect of surgery—the fact that there was a standard framework to the whole thing, so that even when something went wrong the surgical staff still had procedures in place for dealing with it.

Today, however, she felt like the meat in a sandwich. As soon as she'd calmed down and dragged her mind away from Duncan, she had time to think about the encounter with Alex which lay ahead. Nice if Dylan hadn't been part of the equation as well!

Dr Shartles left it to his registrar to complete the final procedure, the patient was wheeled out to

Recovery and Annabelle and the other theatre nurse, Barb Thompson, prepped Theatre Three for the next operation. Annabelle was an experienced scrub nurse, gloved and sterile like the surgeons, and worked closely beside them.

Just beyond the swing doors, she heard Alex's voice, and wasn't surprised at the sharpness in it.

'No, not yet. I have some calls to make first. When Calford gets off the phone.'

So they were both here.

Knots tightened in her temples, and she thought, I wish I was on a beach. With Duncan. I wish we *lived* on a beach. On a tropical island. Eating coconuts and mangoes and yams. I don't want to be here.

'Next patient just got cancelled,' Barb reported. 'Don Laycock. Dr Sturgess's patient. Third time. He's...' She glanced over at Annabelle and quickly amended her sentence. 'Not happy.'

'No, he wouldn't be,' Annabelle agreed. She tried to speak calmly and casually, but it didn't quite come off.

Everyone had already heard about the cancelled wedding when she'd got in this morning, although the hospital friends who'd been at the reception had all told her they wouldn't say anything. She wasn't surprised. It was the kind of news that travelled fast, and perhaps Alex himself had told people. Annabelle hadn't had to deliver the little speech she'd prepared for this morning, and which she knew she'd have garbled despite the preparation.

I'm not the only one who's tense, she realised now. Everyone is wondering how this is going to go.

Badly.

They all knew it as soon as the swing doors crashed open.

'Gram positive cocci in his blood sample,' Alex said. A systemic infection, in other words, disqualifying the patient for surgery. 'I don't know why we have to wait until *now* to hear it. Next patient isn't prepped yet, so I'll be back in half an hour.'

He disappeared again before anyone could acknowledge his words in any way, and he hadn't given the slightest sign that he'd known Annabelle was there. He did know it, though. She was in no doubt of that. In his wake, the swing doors vibrated like drum skins.

The knots in her temples grew tighter.

'Take lunch?' Barb suggested.

'Quickly,' anaesthetist Sharon Curtis agreed. 'Because some people's half-hours are shorter than others.'

She meant Alex, although she was careful not to say so.

Until Friday, Annabelle had rather enjoyed the feeling that she was the only one of the theatre staff to know how different Dr Sturgess could be away from this environment. Now, as she left Theatre and headed for the surgical staff tearoom, she suddenly found herself thinking, But this is the environment where he likes to be. Does he like the excuse to terrorise people, and to know that his whims are law? I think he does...

'Dr Calford, you've heard about Don Laycock getting cancelled?' Barb said.

Dylan had just put down the phone, and joined Annabelle and Barb as they headed down the corridor to the tearoom.

'Yes. Third time.' He nodded. 'Poor guy. He's a nervous patient. I think he felt reprieved when he heard—I was checking out another patient in the next bed at the time—but it just prolongs the agony, since he'll have to key himself up all over again once the infection is dealt with.'

He flicked a quick look across to Annabelle and she went hot. Was he thinking the same thing she was? That the same applied to the way she felt about Alex? Keyed up to stand next to him over an operating table. Half an hour's reprieve before she had to key herself up again.

Just before they reached the tearoom, Dylan held her back with a hand on her arm. She wanted to fight his touch, but knew she'd only draw more attention to the way it affected her.

'Wasn't sure if we'd see you today,' he said.

What was it that Mum had said on Friday night? Oh, that's right… 'Life goes on,' she answered.

'As I told my lawyer this morning,' Dylan said, 'when I accepted Sarah's suggested settlement package.'

The cynical drawl didn't suit him, and Annabelle felt an absurd urge to tell him, Don't judge the whole world differently because of a bad marriage. I hate to see you this way.

She kept her mouth firmly shut, of course.

'Alex knocked back my offer of paying for the reception, by the way,' Dylan continued.

'You didn't seriously think he'd accept?'

'No. I didn't.' He added in a low tone, 'Still wondering what I can get *you* to accept. Something, Annabelle.'

'Nothing,' she countered quickly. 'I don't want it. Just forget it.'

'I'm on standby if you change your mind. Meanwhile, I'm at least taking you out to dinner, OK?'

She shook her head. 'Booked up. Sorry.'

'You need some time to yourself. You're stressed out.'

'I know. But there's no time available.'

'Hmm.' He looked at her narrowly for a moment, then went across to the urn and made himself some coffee, turning his back to her as if she wasn't there.

In well-washed theatre gear, his body was impressive in a way she'd never noticed before, and didn't want to notice now. The muscles in his back were clearly defined and solid, although the total impression was one of athleticism rather than bulk. He moved comfortably. A lean and stretch to the left to reach for a mug, an efficient scoop and flick with the spoon in the coffee-can.

His hair was cut short at the back, and was thick enough to hold its shape without being stubbly or spiky. His nape looked soft and sensitive, the perfect place for a woman's fingers to stroke and linger. When he started humming a chart-topping song tunelessly under his breath, and tapping a bar or two of its beat with his fingers on the counter-top, Annabelle turned firmly away and stopped listening.

It was as if Alex's petulant suspicions about an affair between herself and Dylan had changed something in her own perceptions. In some part of her, an invisible line had been crossed. Dylan wasn't just a colleague any more. For good or ill, their relationship was personal now.

When he sat down, she made her own tea and sat as far from him as she could, pretending to read a magazine while she gulped down her sandwich. It was nothing but pretence. In reality, she noticed every time he re-crossed his legs, and every time he brought his mug to his lips and pouted them a little to drink.

Twenty minutes later, she was back outside Theatre Three and ready to scrub, while an orderly talked to the incoming patient, drowsy from her pre-med.

Alex didn't reappear.

'Does he want us to wait?' Barb asked. 'Do you know, Dr Calford? Dr Curtis? I got the impression…'

No one was sure.

Dylan found himself thinking, Whatever we do, it'll turn out to be wrong.

Not for the first time, he wished that Alex's well-deserved reputation as the best knee surgeon in Queensland hadn't wooed him into coming back here last year to work with the man again. If he'd known Sarah had been on the point of calling it quits with their marriage, he might have gone further afield. There were excellent knee surgeons in Sydney and Melbourne, too. Sarah was the one committed to living in Brisbane, with family here and a career in public relations.

When I'm at Alex's level, I'm not going to waste my own energy and everyone else's in terrorising the staff, he thought. I don't believe people perform better when they're on edge the way we all are today.

Aloud, after another two minutes had ticked by with no senior surgeon in sight, he decreed, 'We'll start. Page him, if necessary, but we shouldn't have to.'

He was just going in for the first incision when Alex appeared at last.

'Go ahead, Dr Calford,' he invited at once, but there was something in his drawling tone which signalled clearly to Dylan that he was on trial with this one. Yes, he'd done the procedure numerous times. Yes, he'd been told by Alex himself that his hip replacement technique was excellent. But every patient was different, and when Alex was in the mood to quibble...

He felt Annabelle beside him, her tension communicated in some mysterious way that he couldn't quite pinpoint. The way she was moving, perhaps. It was more abrupt than usual, and the clatter of the instruments in the trays seemed louder, as if she was fumbling. Normally, her hands were neat and efficient and graceful, unconsciously inviting a man to think about other ways in which she'd use them well.

Dylan wanted to tell her to relax but knew that if he did so, he'd be admitting what everyone already knew but no one wanted to say.

Alex has got us walking on knife blades.

'Hold it, James,' Dylan said to the resident, whose main job was to observe and keep the elderly woman's leg where Dylan wanted it. He gave a more technical instruction about position, and James Nguyen nodded then lifted the inert leg higher and rotated it outward.

'No,' Alex said immediately, and made a minute adjustment. It called Dylan's own positioning into question and left James struggling with taking the heavy weight of the woman's leg at an awkward angle.

Annabelle stared down at the table, the bright operating lights shadowing her face, which was already hard to read because of her mask and the cap that came low on her forehead. As a gesture of support, Dylan nudged his leg against hers, but he should have realised it wouldn't be taken as reassurance.

She moved away at once, and he coached himself, Forget it. Concentrate. Do the job.

The nuances of emotion flying across the operating table were like bats. He wanted to fight them off, but it was better to leave them alone.

Alex kept saying, 'No!' And every time they'd all freeze, until he'd dealt with the alleged mistake. Wrong scalpel. Wrong cement mixture prepared. Wrong this, and wrong that. Dylan's scalp tightened with anger and frustration that he had to keep bottled inside while he went doggedly on with the delicate procedure. The patient was elderly, and wouldn't bounce back easily from a botched job or a persistent infection.

'No, Dr Calford,' Alex said again.

Wouldn't it be nice, though, to shoot my whole career down in flames with one well-aimed fist? Dylan decided. A whole raft of reasons held him back, and he knew that control was the stronger and tougher response. His jaw ached.

Beyond the appalling atmosphere, the procedure itself was actually going well, although an untrained observer would have thought they were witnessing a medical disaster.

And then Annabelle opened the wrong hip pack.

Alex exploded. 'You should have known I'd want the new ceramic hip for this patient,' he shouted. 'And if you didn't know, you should have asked! Do you realise you have just ruined over $3000 worth of equipment? Get the right pack, please, someone, and get it now!'

'I'm sorry, Dr Sturgess.' Annabelle's voice shook.

Barb was already looking for the right hip pack, her movements quick and a little clumsy. The error was as much hers as Annabelle's but, in fact, the fault lay most heavily on Alex's shoulders. He should have made his wishes clear. His staff weren't mind-readers. Dylan hadn't known he was planning to use a ceramic hip today either.

While they waited for Barb, Annabelle stood back, her shoulders held high and tight. Alex was becoming more impatient by the second, and didn't try to hide the fact.

'I can't possibly operate under these conditions,' he said in a cold tone.

Nobody pointed out that he hadn't actually been operating at all. The gleaming instruments were all in Dylan's hands. 'I'll expect a report later, Calford, and I'll expect to be paged if you can't handle the next procedure.'

'Fine. No problem,' Dylan said, without moving his lips.

The senior surgeon walked out as if he hadn't heard.

Sharon controlled a sigh, and after a thunderous and lengthy silence said, 'Anyone hear anything about the cricket?'

'All out,' James answered in a thin voice. 'Can't remember the score.'

'All right, everyone, let's take a deep breath and focus, OK?' Dylan said. 'We all have our off-days. Found that hip pack yet, Barb?'

'Yes, finally.'

'It's no one's fault. I hope we're all clear on that.'

The relief he saw in four sets of eyes, above four disposable masks, confirmed his belief that his, not Alex's, was the better way to get results.

Only fifteen minutes late going off, Annabelle noted with relief as she crossed the main hospital foyer in her street clothes. Felt as if she'd been here for about fourteen hours. A spot high on her spine was burning, her shoulders ached and her stomach rumbled.

But three-fifteen was good. She'd have enough time to do a couple of odd jobs at Mum's before they had to leave for her four-thirty appointment. The traffic was still fairly light, and in the short stretches when it wasn't, Annabelle tried the method that Vic always used to urge on her.

'*Visualise* what you want, and it'll happen.'

OK, the three cars ahead are going to turn right at the next light, and I'll be able to overtake that truck…

For Annabelle, at least, it never worked.

At Mum's they made a list of the shopping Annabelle needed to do—some for Mum, some for herself and Duncan—and she watered the plants on the little balcony. She saw Mum's inhaler sitting on the coffee-table…and an open packet of cigarettes on the kitchen window-sill.

She didn't say anything about them, and neither did Mum.

They'd had a huge blow-up on the subject after Vic's death. Mum had given up six years ago, after starting in the swinging sixties and smoking forty a day for the next thirty-two years, but after the news had come about Vic, she'd started again, just a couple a day. Annabelle had exploded when she'd first found the evidence, about three weeks after Vic's funeral.

'I've lost Dad, and I've lost my sister, and now you're doing your best to shorten *your* life, so that I'll lose you, too? Am I the only person with any sanity around here?'

'I lost her, too!' Helen yelled back. 'And I lost Bill. Don't you think that I feel weak and guilty for needing this? But I can hardly get through the days at the moment. Leave me alone!'

Annabelle almost…*almost*…stormed out. A second before slamming Mum's front door, she turned back. They were both in tears. Hers were the first tears she had been able to shed since the news had come. The first tears she'd *let* herself shed, with so much else to do, and in her care a sad, confused baby boy who'd just learned to walk.

She and Helen held out their arms to each other, and sobbed and rocked in each other's embrace for a long time. They were closer from that day on, with a relationship that was richer and deeper, and the closeness gave them a lot of courage.

'We'd better get going, Mum,' Annabelle said at just after four. Then she watched as her mother picked up the inhaler but left the cigarettes where they were.

Dr Badger was on time today. Mum needed her routine appointments with him fairly often these days. He tested her lung function before and after she used the inhaler, and checked for evidence of infection or the dangerous pockets of trapped air which were called bullae.

The news today was mixed. Mum was worried that her inhaler had been losing its effect over the past few days. It contained a bronchodilator which opened her airways as much as her disease allowed.

But Dr Badger shook his head. 'No, I think you'll find that's not the problem.' He was a rather ponderous man in his late fifties, and spoke slowly.

'What do you think is going on, then, Dr Badger?' Annabelle asked. Helen always preferred that she come into the doctor's office too, trusting her to later interpret anything that she hadn't understood.

'You've got a chest infection, Mrs Drew, so we'll treat you for that, and I'll see you again next week.'

He wrote out a script for oral antibiotics, and they made a follow-up appointment with the receptionist. With the prescription to pick up and shopping to do, while Mum waited in the car, Annabelle didn't reach Gumnut Playcare until ten past six.

Duncan was one of just three children left at the child-care centre, and he wasn't playing with the other two, who were a couple of years older, but was slumped on a beanbag, kicking his heels on the floor. Bored? Angry? Lonely? Possibly all three. The afternoon staff were clearing up for the day and paid him no attention.

When he saw Annabelle, he was on his feet in seconds, eager to hurl himself into her arms. Feeling his warm little body against her, and his soft hair tickling her cheek, she hugged him tightly, whispered, 'I missed you today,' and almost cried.

'Go inna pool?' he asked at once, and although it was the last thing she felt like, she promised him they'd have a lovely cool swim as soon as they got home.

CHAPTER FOUR

THE doorbell rang just as Annabelle was poised on the lip of the pool in her colourful bathing suit. Duncan hopped impatiently beside her, ready for his first exuberant leap into the water and into her arms as soon as she'd eased her way down the steps.

'Let's see who that is,' she told him, and hefted him onto her hip so they'd actually have a chance of reaching the front door before the person gave up and left again. Duncan wasn't very goal-oriented about the doorbell.

When she saw Dylan standing there, she wished she hadn't taken the trouble.

'You said you weren't available to go out, so I thought I'd better bring dinner in,' he said, lifting several bulging plastic shopping bags in each hand.

'You're not going to leave this alone, are you?'

'Not yet,' he agreed calmly.

'Even if I tell you that I'm—'

'Stop!' He stepped through the doorway and dumped the shopping bags just inside her tiny entrance hall. 'I warn you, I've prepared for all the excuses. I've brought groceries, in case you had to go shopping.'

Duncan was already examining the contents of the bags.

'No, I've just been shopping.'

'And…' He bent to a vinyl athletic bag at his feet, and she was astonished to see him pull out a hair-dryer, a brush and bottles of shampoo and conditioner.

'*What?*'

'Classic female excuse number three. If you're washing your hair tonight, I've brought the necessary equipment.'

He grinned a cool, lazy, challenging grin as he flourished the hair-dryer in his hand, and suddenly she was laughing helplessly, laughing until tears flooded her eyes, laughing despite the fact that it wasn't all that funny, laughing just because it was a relief to let go and feel silly for once.

'Sorry, wrong brand of shampoo?' he suggested, as she clung, weak-kneed, to the doorframe.

Duncan, who was still examining the plastic bags, happily announced, 'Chippies! Yummy!' And started laughing, too.

'The girl next door provided the salon supplies for me,' Dylan said.

'I'll just bet she did, Dylan Calford! You're not proving an easy man to say no to. The shampoo is…' Annabelle lifted her hand helplessly '…fine.' It was a far more expensive brand than she ever bought for herself. 'I'm sorry, I think I must have needed that, or something. The laughing, I mean.'

'I can imagine that you did. Are you going to let me all the way in?' He was still poised with his heels on the doorstep.

'I'll have to, won't I?' But it wasn't nearly as belligerent a statement as it could have been in a different tone.

Annabelle began looking around for something on which to wipe her streaming eyes, and realised that all she had on was her bathing suit. She used the heel of her hand instead. 'Um, Duncan and I were just going for a swim.'

'So I see.'

'I'd invite you to join us, only—'

'I don't have a suit.'

'And I don't have any spares.'

'Might not fit, even if you did.'

'I meant spare *men's*.'

She hadn't missed the sweeping glance that trailed over her figure, on show in the sleek, close-fitting swimsuit, and it disturbed her. She knew why he was here. The 'making amends' thing. And she was starting to understand that it was best to let him get it out of his system.

But there was something more, and it wasn't coming from him, it was coming from her. She didn't want to be aware of him like this. Growing hot when he came near. Conscious of her own body—of its curves and its pulse points and its position in space. Enjoying the zestful atmosphere of his company, even when she was angry with him.

Nothing could come of it. It was simply a nuisance, and when she'd already known him for three and a half years without feeling this way she ought to be able to get rid of it quickly.

'Maybe after you've been for yours, and you're getting Duncan dressed, I could skinny-dip for a few minutes,' he suggested. 'It's fairly private out there, if I remember.'

'Yes,' she agreed, *not* thinking about it.

Dylan Calford, naked in her pool, powering through the water like a shark. Water making a glistening film over his skin. Tan lines low on his back and high on his thighs, and between them…

'It's very private,' she went on quickly. 'You can't even see it from inside the house.'

'First, though, I'll get this lot into the kitchen.'

'What on earth have you brought?'

'Take-away Thai, and I didn't know what you liked, so I got a lot of different dishes. And wine. Red and white. Basic groceries to knock the shopping excuse on the head.' He stopped and looked at her. 'Although I think perhaps you're a little less angry with me than you were.'

'I'm not sure who I'm angry with today after the way Alex behaved this afternoon,' she admitted.

Shouldn't have admitted it, and waited, holding her breath uncomfortably, for him to comment. He didn't. Which was nice of him.

She and Duncan had their usual noisy swim. Dylan didn't appear until she'd said, 'Three more jumps, Duncan.'

Standing with his arms resting on the top of the pool gate and a grin on his face, he watched the three jumps, and the 'one more lucky last' that Annabelle always agreed to.

'There are spare towels in the bin, just there,' she told Dylan, and then carried a towel-wrapped Duncan inside to give him a quick rinse in the shower and get him into his pyjamas.

Just before the veranda door closed behind her, Annabelle heard the sound of a resonant splash. Dylan—naked—had just dived in.

The kitchen was an Aladdin's cave of new groceries, she found when she arrived there to heat up some leftover spaghetti and a plate of fruit for Duncan's dinner. Dylan must have brought at least two more loads of shopping bags up from the car, and he'd unpacked it all and wadded the bags together, making it impossible, or at least difficult, for her to say, No, take it back. I didn't need you to do this.

In the pantry, there were cans of tomatoes and soup and corn, packets of spaghetti and biscuits and tea, boxes of cereal, jars of peanut butter and curry sauce. In the fridge there were tubs of yoghurt and blocks of cheese, and in the freezer there were packets of sausages, minced beef, chicken and steak.

In the oven, on a very low heat, he'd stacked the Thai take-away containers to keep them warm. A quick look told her there were dishes enough to freeze later tonight and fall back on for half a dozen meals over the next few weeks, a reprieve from the 'What will we eat tonight?' dilemma that plagued her every evening as she drove home. Duncan liked spicy food.

Annabelle immediately started her usual obsessive, anxious calculations. This will keep us going on basics and freezer supplies for months. I'll halve my food bills. I can pay the credit card bill down. I can take some of this over to Mum's...

Mum could only afford to stay in her unit because it was all paid off, and she had to manage her cash flow as carefully as Annabelle did.

Then she went beyond the initial relief of it and rebelled.

She must not let her immediate need cloud her broader perspective. She couldn't let Dylan think that it was OK to do this. It wasn't. On a practical level, she might need his guilt offerings, but she didn't want them. After the drama of Alex's walkout on Friday night, 'want' was winning over 'need' this week. For once, she would rebel. For once, she would act on

selfish feelings and high-minded, *expensive* principles, instead of making a calculated sacrifice.

Without stopping to think, she strapped Duncan
into his high chair, gave him a couple of crackers and
some juice to tide him over and marched straight out
to the pool.

Dylan didn't have a tan line at all. His body—or
the back of it, at least—was pale golden brown all
over.

'Sorry. Later,' she blurted, and turned on her heel.

'Is there a problem?' he said behind her.

She turned again. It wasn't a very natural movement. Much too slow. Breath held too tightly. He had
reached the far end of the pool and was standing up,
waist deep, using his hands like a towel to wipe the
water off his face.

'It can wait,' she answered.

'Can it? I heard the door slam, and then the pool
gate, and you stood there at the edge of the water like
my old school swimming coach, about to blow his
whistle and yell.'

The water, which had been churning in his wake,
began to settle and grow still, and since Annabelle
had a very good relationship with the man at the local
pool supply shop, its chemical balance was perfect
and it was crystal clear.

'Nothing. I just— I wanted to— Um, thank you for
the groceries. And the take-away. Don't do it again,
Dylan, I mean it. If you were planning to, that is. But
please, please, don't.'

Crystal clear. Dylan didn't have a tan line in front
either.

'Annabelle—'

'Keep on with your lap swimming, and we'll talk about it later.'

He shrugged. 'If you think there's something to talk about. I put the take-away containers in the—'

'I saw.'

Still and aqua-tinted and completely translucent. Dylan himself probably didn't realise quite how translucent. He had the western sun in his eyes, and the light bouncing into his face off the bright surface of the water.

'Just come inside when you're ready,' she said. 'I'm giving Duncan something else to eat tonight. And I'd better—'

'Yes, go and feed him. I'll be out in a few minutes.'

He launched himself into a strong crawl towards her, his shoulders and arms breaking the water smoothly and his feet making it bubble like a volcanic hot spring behind. In between the shoulders at one end and the feet at the other, she saw the tight curves of the human body's largest muscles. Nope. He really didn't have a tan line at all.

Duncan had finished eating by the time Dylan came in. He was dressed in the smart grey business trousers and shirt he'd been wearing before, but now the shirt-sleeves were rolled to his elbows and he'd left the top two buttons unfastened. His hair was damp, vigorously towelled and uncombed, so that it stood up a little messily on his head.

He didn't seem in a hurry to fix the problem, but Annabelle felt her own fingers itching to do the job. Just a little finger-combing back from his forehead, and a stroke or two down towards the water-cooled nape of his neck.

I can't afford to notice these things about him, she

thought. I can't feel like this. It's stupid. The kind of complication I absolutely do not need!

Duncan yawned, and she looked at the clock. It was after eight, and he was ready for bed.

Dylan read the yawn and Annabelle's glance correctly. 'Yes, go ahead,' he said. 'Put him to bed, and we'll eat afterwards.'

She nodded. 'He's always happy to go, which I'm thankful for after some of the stories I hear from other parents about tantrums over b-e-d.'

'All children have their redeeming features, as I understand it,' he teased.

'He's great. You're great, aren't you, Duncan?' she asked him, and he nodded happily.

He was tucked up in bed, after a story about trucks, ten minutes later.

This left Annabelle alone with Dylan, Thai food and wine at the table he'd set on the back veranda. About the only things missing were candles and flowers, but the lights by the pool, shining back through the tropical greenery and edging the white frangipani flowers with radiance, were a more than adequate substitute. The atmosphere was far more indulgent to the senses than Annabelle wanted it to be.

'Don't do this again,' she told Dylan abruptly. 'Please.'

'You said that,' he answered, 'as if you're worried I'm about to make you my good deed for the month.'

'And aren't you? I can see the evidence right now.'

He laughed. 'You have a point. But if you're telling me not to…'

'I'm telling you not to, Dylan.'

'OK.' He took the lids off the containers, filling her nostrils with the sweet, hot aromas of chilli and lime and coconut and curry. 'Dig in. Since it's a one-off event, we may as well enjoy it to the full.'

Dylan opened the chilled white wine and filled the stemmed glasses with liquid the colour of pale straw, as clear and inviting as the water in the pool. He lifted his glass in a gesture which invited Annabelle to do the same, and they moved to clink them together, eyes fixed on each other. How had that happened? When had she looked up at him?

'To changed plans,' he said, then pulled back and took his glass away at the last second. Annabelle's hand jerked a little, and she felt foolishly deprived, like Duncan if his ice cream dropped off its wooden stick halfway to his mouth. 'Or are you not yet ready to make a toast like that?' Dylan asked.

Annabelle put her glass down hard. 'You're arrogant, aren't you, Dylan Calford? Beyond a bit of guilt at the inconvenience of your timing, you still think you saved me.'

'And you don't agree? Even after today?'

'Of course Alex behaved badly. Anyone would have. It was an emotional situation for both of us. For everyone in the room! I got my head down, and I handled it.'

'You shouldn't have to. You weren't the one who called off the wedding. He's the one who's made a mountain out of a molehill.'

'Easy to dictate how other people should behave when you've never been in a situation anything like that.'

She saw his jaw tighten, heard the staccato hiss of his breath and thought, Good one, Annabelle.

She knew his divorce had rocked him. Everyone knew it, since he hadn't tried particularly hard to hide the fact. She remembered a couple of times when she'd been in the nurse's change-room and he hadn't known anyone was there—or he hadn't cared. There was a wall-mounted phone in the corridor just outside, and she'd heard him talking to Sarah.

Not the words. She'd tried not to listen. But the tone and the cadence of a man's voice gave away a lot. Low and emotional, tight and strident with anger. Once his pager had gone off and they'd both been called into emergency surgery. That time, she *had* heard.

'It's urgent, Sarah, so I have to go. Can we talk about this later? Please? It's a bit unfair, isn't it, to just—? Well, you knew that when we got married. I didn't hide it from you. Look, anyway. Later. No? OK. OK, Sarah, but don't *ever* accuse me of not being prepared to talk!'

When Annabelle came out of the change-room, he was still pacing the far end of the corridor, his capable body angular and tightly wound, and she didn't even think he'd seen her. Ten minutes later, in surgery, he was cool and controlled as always—a team leader, never a whip-cracker.

'I'm sorry,' she apologised now. 'That was overstepping—'

'It's all right. We've started doing that to each other a bit, haven't we?' he agreed, and the way he watched her was like a flood of hot sunshine, or a cloud of fresh scent. 'Minding each other's business instead of our own.'

They both knew why. They didn't need to say it. It was like a secret that only the two of them knew. Linking them together. Pulling them together. Tangling them in sinuous, silky cords of shared awareness. If she'd been doubtful, earlier, about the extent to which he felt this, too, she wasn't doubtful any more. They wanted each other. They desired each other. And she couldn't remember when she'd ever felt like this before.

She must have. Surely. But it didn't feel familiar. It felt unique, and she knew she hadn't felt it for Alex.

Should she have felt it for a man she'd been ready to marry? Or was the quieter, less physical attraction between two people more reliable, stronger and more enduring? She didn't know.

All she did know was that she didn't want to feel this way about Dylan Calford. Not now. Not when it only served to confuse her.

'We can stop,' she said. 'We can stop doing it. Putting our noses into each other's business, I mean. And everything else. Heaven knows, I don't want to. I'm not remotely happy about being in this situation. Without your interference on Friday, none of this would be happening.'

Now, there's an appealing thought, Dylan decided.

He wasn't ready for this either. Didn't want to analyse the whys and wherefores too closely. He just knew he wasn't. Not yet. He was too bruised, too cynical, too battle-wearied. He needed to regain a little of his faith in the human race. And a nice woman like Annabelle Drew didn't deserve to be picked up for a sizzling yet casual affair and then cast aside—which was about all he felt capable of doing at the moment.

The growing chemistry between them suggested she'd be great at the sizzling part. It was the casting aside that wouldn't work.

A week ago, he'd never thought of sex and Sister

Drew in the same breath. Now he wondered how he'd ever be able to separate them again. Across the table, bathed in a light that was far too mellow and golden to be safe for either of them, she had started to eat. She was taking refuge in it, looking down at her plate, as if avoiding eye contact with each other might help.

So far, however, it wasn't helping *him*. The light made her hair shine, and the dipped gaze silhouetted the black satin length of her eyelashes against her flushed cheeks. She lifted a forkful of chicken and rice to her lips and tucked a strand of hair behind her ear, and every movement she made mesmerised him and had him dwelling on the other things that hands and lips and hair could do. The things they could do in bed.

'Mmm, it's good,' she said, and her mouth made a pouting kiss shape on the last word.

Dylan's brain went foggy. She was talking about the meal, not the hot images that filled his mind. He tried to say something helpful, like which restaurant he'd picked it up from, and what this particular dish was called, but neither of those details had stuck. As for something a little more ambitious and intellectual...

'Spicy food really works in the hot weather, doesn't it?' he said at last.

Oh, brilliant!

But she smiled and seized on the topic, although it didn't deserve such zealous attention. 'Yes, like hot tea.'

'Or beer so cold it makes your forehead ache.'

'Or a cold shower. Do you ever do that on a hot night? I don't dry myself, I just stand in front of an electric fan before I get dressed until I'm *freezing*, and then I float around with some actual energy for about twenty minutes until I get sticky again.'

'I swim at night a lot,' he said.

'You have a pool, too?' Brisbane's back gardens were thickly dotted with them, in a climate which permitted outdoor swimming most of the year round.

'Yes, very private, like yours,' he answered, 'only my privacy comes from the courtyard wall, not from jungle greenery like this. I don't really have a back garden, just a landscaped pool surround. I've swum at four in the morning on a hot night. If I can't sleep, or if I get home after a call-out to the hospital.'

'I love swimming at night,' she agreed.

She glanced across at the pool, and he wondered if she'd swim tonight after he'd gone. Would she bother to put on her suit, or would she simply peel off the skirt, the clingy, scoop-necked top and whatever she wore beneath it and slip, seal-like, into the blue water?

He spent the rest of the meal using conversation to fight the vivid pictures in his mind, and they ended up having a rambling talk about a dozen different things that went on for at least an hour and a half.

'Well,' Annabelle finally said.

This was unbelievably nice. Two glasses of wine to cool the pleasurable bite of the spice in her mouth. Coffee, to go with the French apple tart she hadn't spotted in the fridge earlier. The table was a mess of leftovers, but it didn't matter. Whether it was fatigue or wine—probably both—she felt deliciously light-headed.

And happy. Stupidly happy, really, under the circumstances.

Must remind Mum about taking her antibiotic. What if she needs a second course?

'You're *rounder* than I'd thought you'd be, Dylan,' she told him a little unsteadily, to cut off the drone of worries in her head.

'And you've had too much wine.'

'No… Yes,' she admitted. 'A little. Your fault. You kept pouring it. One glass is all I'm good for, especially when I'm tired. I've had two tonight.'

The bottle still had a couple of centimetres left in the bottom of it.

'And I'm round?'

'Rounded, I meant. Orthopaedic surgeons are supposed to be more predictable. Narrower, or something. More focused.'

'Are they?'

'Well, you know, playing the banjo. It's supposed to be golf. Something with networking possibilities.'

'Don't like golf. And there was absolutely no point in me taking up an instrument I had to get serious about. My friends are very generous to let me do the odd practice with their band.'

'And some of that teen stuff you told me about.'

'Running away to try and join the navy when I was fourteen and a half? I was miserable when my father's company first sent him and my mother here. Thought I could jump ship in San Diego or Hawaii and hitch back home to Illinois. Five years later, though, when they got sent home again…'

'You didn't want to go back.'

'I was at university here, and I had a girlfriend.'

'What happened to her?'

'We reached an amicable parting of the ways a year

or two later. Long time ago. Don't know what she's doing now.'

Alex. What was *he* doing now? She should have been with him tonight, enjoying the first week of their marriage, talking about moving more of her things to his place and getting a real estate agent in to look at this house. Instead, she was still here. Alex had had several boxes of her belongings delivered here while she'd been at work, and they were piled in her small third bedroom, awaiting her attention.

And yet she had another man in the house.

Annabelle saw that the watch on Dylan's wrist read ten forty-five, and her feeling of light-headed contentment fled, the way a pleasant dream sometimes fled when her alarm went off, way too early in the morning to be civilised. She stood up.

'Dylan, I'm sorry, I hadn't realised it was getting so late.'

'I had,' he drawled.

He stood up, too, not in a flurry like she had, but lazily, reluctantly.

'Why didn't you say something?'

'I was still debating which thing I should say.'

The dangerous glint in his dark eyes warned her not to ask about what he considered his choices to have been.

'Are you in surgery tomorrow?' she asked quickly.

As an orthopaedic registrar, he usually was. At this stage in his career, he would spend around thirty hours a week performing a wide range of procedures, and that didn't count his extensive periods of time on call for emergencies. If Annabelle managed to move her hours to nights, as she was hoping to do—she

was seeing the unit co-ordinator about it tomorrow—
she would still see Dylan fairly often.

She'd see less of Alex, who only came in at night
when Dylan called on him. She wasn't yet sure how
she would feel about this and, in the greater scheme
of things, it wasn't important. The goal was to have
more time with Duncan and Mum.

'Yes, I'm in surgery,' Dylan was saying. 'I'm not
sure what's scheduled tomorrow.'

'We'll find out. In about eight hours. Which is too
soon.' She stifled a yawn, and saw him touch a hand
to the outside of his hip pocket to confirm that he had
his keys.

'I'll see you in the morning,' he said.

He didn't offer to help clear up, which she was
grateful for. She began to follow him to the door, not
quite shooing him out but close. He didn't resist, but
then, at the last moment, he turned. 'Throw those
empty containers out, OK?'

Annabelle hadn't expected it, and almost barged
into him, bringing herself to a halt on wobbly feet
just a fraction of a second before they made contact.
His hand shot out to her shoulder, heavy and warm,
and he muttered, 'Sorry. I didn't realise you were
right behind me.'

'I'm fine.' He still had his hand on her shoulder,
and her breath felt fluttery.

'Don't wash them out, Annabelle.'

'I'm sorry?' She'd totally lost track of what he was
saying.

'I'm not making sense.' The front hallway was
dark, and his face was shadowy and hard to read.
Only his eyes seemed clear, with fragments of light

from the street reflected deep within them. 'The take-away containers.'

'Oh, right.'

'Don't wash them out to store Duncan's snacks in, or something. You were going to, weren't you?'

She nodded ruefully, and he smiled. 'Thought so. You try too hard. You're too good.'

'I'm not.'

'Yes, you are. I shouldn't be doing this.' He gave her shoulder a little squeeze, and she felt his other hand come to rest on her hip, caressing it with light, slow strokes.

'I'm not too good, Dylan. Don't…make assumptions.' They were standing impossibly close now, looking into each other's faces. His mouth was just a grey blur in the darkness, his nose and his cheekbones highlighted by a diffuse streak of light.

Time seemed to stand still. Annabelle heard the house creak, heard the soft rhythm of Dylan's breathing.

The possibility of a kiss made the air around them as thick and sultry as the air before a summer storm. Her heart throbbed, slow and heavy, and deep in her stomach there was an ache that was half pleasure, half pain. She waited, wanting it and not wanting it at the same time, not yet physically able to tear herself away from the powerful aura of their awareness.

Almost in a trance, she reached up, wanting to trace the line of his lips with her fingers. Was his mouth really as close as it seemed? Was it warm and trembling, as hers was?

'Dylan…' she whispered.

But before she could reach him, his hand captured hers and closed around it. He stroked her knuckles with the ball of his thumb, tangled his fingers in hers and made them dance with his—a slow, seductive dance that sent thrills of need flooding up her arm. She could feel his thighs against hers, hard and heavy and warm.

Annabelle shivered, and knew that he would understand exactly what the convulsive movement meant. She ached for him. She wanted him. His touch and his heat, his breath on her skin, and his whispered words, low and husky, filling her mouth as they kissed.

But it didn't happen. Nothing specific or concrete broke the moment. Dylan dropped his hand from her hip, just as she dragged herself deliberately back from the giddy brink of what she felt. They each recognised the decision that the other one had made, and saw the tangled feelings reflected in each other's face.

'I'll see you tomorrow, Sister Drew,' Dylan said lightly, and ducked quickly through the front door he'd just opened, while Annabelle was still struggling for an acceptable, neutral reply.

CHAPTER FIVE

DYLAN'S back ached sharply, low in his spine.

A couple of friends had invited him for a sailing weekend and they'd gone down to Stradbroke Island. They'd taken advantage of summer's light evenings to head out straight after work on Friday afternoon and hadn't moored back at the marina until after dark on Sunday night.

Two long days, three late nights, a lot of stretching and pulling on ropes, a lot of bending and twisting in cramped cabins. They'd fished and barbecued, swum off the side of the boat before breakfast and had had a few beers at sunset. Dylan had been looking forward to the trip since Chris had mooted the idea some weeks ago, and he'd begged Chris and David to schedule it for a weekend when he wasn't on call.

It was the first break he'd taken in months, and the first stretch of free time in which his mind hadn't been dominated by painful, repetitive, hostile thoughts about Sarah. It had felt like a celebration, and the marker of a new and better stage in his life. Some of his battle-weariness had healed and faded.

He could look around and see that there *were* happy marriages. David and his wife had been together for fourteen years, and you could hear how much they loved each other just from the way David spoke to Liz on the phone.

But now my back is killing me, Dylan thought. I feel like an old man!

He was annoyed at himself. Firstly, because he'd been so sure he was fit, since he swam almost every day and jogged or hiked when he could. Secondly, because he'd been wrong about his fitness, and now he was paying for it.

The pain was surprisingly sharp, surprisingly intense and extremely inconvenient only a couple of hours into a long day of surgery. He was handling all of Alex's list today, since everything was routine. Alex was getting back a day late from a conference. This placed an added weight of responsibility on Dylan's own shoulders…but at least it spared all of them the moody behaviour Alex was still acting out, four and a half weeks after he'd walked out of his own wedding.

So far, the atmosphere in the operating theatre had been relaxed and pleasant this morning. If their current patient was numbered amongst those rare people who remained aware under general anaesthesia, he would have nothing to complain about. No one yelled. No one swore. No one said anything offensive—no jokes about a patient's cellulite or ugly toenails.

Sharon Curtis talked about a new restaurant. Circulating nurse Barbara Thompson outlined her holiday plans. Dylan asked Annabelle about her weekend. Casually. He always did it casually, and if she guessed that he was still looking for ways to make her life a little easier, she didn't let on.

Why should she? He hadn't succeeded in his mission to any significant extent. Once, during the past three weeks, she had let him buy her lunch—but only because he'd offered to buy Barb's at the same time. Annabelle had also mentioned that her car needed some work, and he'd recommended the place where he had his own vehicle serviced. Later, he had phoned the head mechanic and asked him to look out for her.

'Do me a favour, OK?'

'Tell me what it is first, Dr Calford!'

'If the bill is more than a hundred dollars or so, leave some of the items off her statement and charge them to my account.'

'No problem.'

The invoice he had received a few days later told him he'd saved her a whole thirty-seven dollars and eighty-eight cents.

As a way of easing the economic burden that had fallen onto Annabelle because she hadn't married Alex Sturgess, Dylan was barely making a dent. Should he leave the whole thing alone? Put it down to an over-developed sense of responsibility on his part, and ignore it until it went away?

And what about that moment—that very long, slow, intense moment—four weeks ago, when they'd almost kissed? Where did that fit in?

Today, Dylan could only file it under I for Inconvenient. He didn't want it. Not yet. Not with someone he had to see every day, and the kind of woman he had to take very seriously or not take at all. Life had been a lot simpler four and a half weeks ago, when he hadn't known what Sister Annabelle Drew looked like in a wedding gown and a bathing suit. He wished he'd never found out.

'Want to tell me how we got to this point with this patient?' he asked the resident, in an effort to distract himself from the pain of his back and the unwanted pleasure of watching the way Annabelle's body moved beneath the soft fabric of her green surgical gear.

'You mean the whole history?' James Nguyen said.

'Quick summary, from when he got carried off the rugby field, with his knee packed in ice.' ·

'OK. Well, I'd guess that was probably some kind of twisting injury.'

'Yep, a high-grade synovial tear.'

'And you would have had him in for pinhole surgery. Fibreoptic instruments inserted into the joint.'

'And what did we do?'

'Shaved the detached tissue and sucked it out,' James said promptly.

'Graphic, but correct.'

'But obviously that wasn't enough?'

'No, we found evidence of a big cruciate tear, quite a mess.'

'So we had to actually open up the knee.'

'Which is what we're doing now. Have a look.' Dylan leaned forward a little, and a fresh spasm of agony attacked him. His hand tensed and shook for a moment, and he hoped no one had seen. 'See how I'm going to shift the leg now? Or rather, get you to shift it and keep it there.'

'That's a better angle, isn't it?'

'Gets to be instinctive after a while.'

In the half-second left before he touched scalpel to flesh to make the cut, Dylan flashed a quick look at Annabelle. If anyone guessed that he was having trouble and pain, it would be her. Nothing to do with the chemistry that had built between them lately, but purely because she was such a cool-headed and experienced theatre nurse.

Her brown eyes met his, but he couldn't read her

expression. She looked as composed as ever. She wasn't frowning. Not that he could see below the blue line of her mask anyway.

His own face felt as tightly screwed up as a piece of unwanted paper and he felt himself sweating. Great! Just great! His body was paying for its excesses just as surely as this patient was paying for his years as a professional rugby player. So much for new beginnings!

But I'm only thirty-three! Dylan thought. The weekend wasn't *that* physical, was it?

The rugby player's knee was a mess, they found. Much worse than Dylan had expected it to be. From the history reported by the patient, he remembered that there had been some knee trouble a few seasons earlier. 'Nothing big. Didn't stop me from playing,' Jason Gregory had said.

Perhaps he should have stopped, however, because playing with the damaged knee had made it a lot worse. There was extensive damage to the bone surface now, with some necrosis—death, in layman's terms—at the ends of both major leg bones.

Dylan glanced at the patient's face, looking peaceful, slack and unaware beneath the uncompromising glare of the overhead lights. Although slightly distorted by the tube protruding from the man's mouth, it was a strong and well-proportioned face, attached to a powerhouse body. Jason Gregory had appeared on magazine covers more than once as sporting hero, hunky pin-up and family man. By all accounts, he was a decent guy, a faithful husband, a keen father and a real team player.

But he would need a complete knee reconstruction, and he would never play professional rugby again.

And I'm going to be the one to give him the news, Dylan realised. How's he going to take it?

At his age, a player of his calibre could reasonably expect another five years in the game. Had he invested his earnings well? Had he considered his future? Not all former players could make it as coaches or commentators. Not all of them had good heads for business, or a second skill they could turn to once their playing days were over.

How did a man deal with having to give up the career he loved, the vocation that had done so much to make him who he was? When it was gone, what was left?

'Here's something that didn't show up during the earlier surgery,' Dylan told the resident. He indicated the extensive areas of bone damage, the necrotic ends and the mess of injuries to the ligaments.

The very young-looking Dr Nguyen whistled. 'What are we going to do?'

'Patch it up for now and plan a complete reconstruction for later. There's no choice. Get in closer and have a look, because it's a degree of damage you might not get to see again for a while.'

Dylan stepped sideways to make more room for the junior surgeon. As he bent over the surgical field, he felt his back burn and spasm with pain once more.

Annabelle *had* noticed something of what he was feeling.

Dylan wasn't certain of this until two hours later, after Jason Gregory had left Recovery to return to his private room in the orthopaedic ward. In the interim, Dylan had done a routine knee replacement on an elderly woman. He felt exhausted from the effort of battling the pain, and more exhausted from the effort of hiding it. It had subsided now, fortunately.

His fears hadn't. He'd chewed painkillers like caramel toffees after Jason Gregory's surgery, and they'd kicked in about an hour ago. Painkillers weren't an ongoing solution, however. What was going on in his body?

'Are you OK, Dylan?' Annabelle fixed him with her big brown eyes as he poured himself a brimming mug of tea. He had the vague notion that the drink would be soothing, and definitely didn't want the stimulant effect of coffee, or its bitter taste in his mouth.

'I'm fine,' he answered.

He *was* fine now, physically, thanks to the painkillers. He'd only taken them for the sake of his performance in surgery. Couldn't risk freezing or doubling up or getting distracted when he had an open knee or hip on the table in front of him and a whole team of people taking their cues from his own performance.

'You looked concerned back there,' Annabelle persisted. 'Was it Jason Gregory's knee? You weren't expecting he would need a total reconstruction, were you?'

'No, I wasn't, but when we opened up the knee and I saw what it looked like, it didn't make sense to consider anything else. You heard what I was saying to James.'

He leaned against the counter-top, partly to get himself safely out of her aura and partly to test whether his back would behave. It did. The painkillers? Or his cautious movement?

Annabelle's aura was another matter. No woman

should smell that good after four hours of surgery. A little steamy, because it was hot and she'd worked hard, but still clean and sweet, like soap and flowers.

'Will he be able to play again?' she asked.

'Realistically? No, he won't,' Dylan answered. 'Not professionally. Some players might get bull-headed about it and try.'

She had her hair twisted into a knot on the top of her head, and a couple of the pins were coming loose. Any minute now it would tumble down to her shoulders, releasing its scent of shampoo. No, OK, she'd felt that it was about to fall. She was reaching up to push the pins back in. The soft green fabric of her top moved across her breasts and he had to fight not to watch. He focused on her face, which wasn't any less attractive than the rest of her body but a lot more acceptable as the object of a man's gaze.

'Playing professionally is all that counts at his level,' she was saying. 'How are you going to tell him?'

'Straight. No ifs or buts. The way I hope someone would tell me if I were in the same position.' A small, distracting throb of fear ran through him. 'I don't want him thinking he's got a chance at one of those one-in-a-million medical miracles they make TV movies about. I'll tell him why, and what would happen if he tried, and why he can't exercise to compensate, and what will happen if there's damage to the other knee as well.'

'And then you'll let him go away and try to put his life back together.'

'Are you saying I should do it differently? Or that I should do more? I think it would be wrong to encourage him to play again. To hold out false hope for him, and risk even worse damage.'

'No, I'm not questioning any of that. But you look as if you want to do more, as if this has hit you quite hard. Is it because he's such a star player?'

No, it's because my back is killing me. Like a sixty-five-year-old man who overdid the pruning and fertilising in his rose garden on the weekend.

It had better not be the start of a pattern! he threatened inwardly, not knowing where to direct his anger. It had better not get any worse!

'When someone's profession is such a big thing in his life, it's always going to be hard,' he answered Annabelle, his voice a little rougher than usual. 'Nothing to do with being a star. It's the ramifications. What if he's…' he cleared his throat '…not good at anything else? What if he's left with no belief in himself?'

Annabelle nodded, moved by the way Dylan spoke with such blunt feeling. She reached for a clean mug, draining upside down on the sink, then watched covertly as he strode across to the fridge, opened the door and hunted for the milk.

He was moving a little stiffly today. His usual animal-like ease with his body seemed to be missing. She remembered the way he'd swum in her pool, tan-line free, and wondered, Is it because of me? I feel as if I move in an unnatural way when I'm around him, too. That stupid moment four weeks ago when I thought we were going to kiss… I think about it— relive it—every time I get within a metre of him, and that happens too often!

Three or four days a week, five or six hours a day, in surgery.

He still had his back to her, standing in front of the fridge. Beneath the hospital green scrub pants, she could see the faint dark shadow of his black under-wear—or maybe it was navy—and the edge of a white T-shirt, coming untucked at his waist. It re-vealed a small, crooked triangle of smooth, beach-brown skin.

He had one elbow propped against the top rim of the fridge, and with the other hand he was probing a spot low on his spine, as if he was testing a bruise. After a few more seconds, he reached cautiously for the milk.

She almost said something, teased him about over-doing it on the weekend, but then he turned and his expression was so preoccupied and closed that she didn't dare to say anything at all.

'Nothing's come up yet,' the unit co-ordinator, Ruth Stacey, told Annabelle half an hour later in her private office. 'You're highly trained and you work in a spe-cialised field, which means it's not easy to move you around.'

'That's what I wanted to say.' Annabelle sat up straighter, then leaned forward. She tried to sound ef-ficient, rather than as if she was begging, although the latter was closer to the truth. 'I'd be willing to switch to night relief work, and just go where I'm needed, for the sake of changing my hours. I know I haven't done general ward nursing or obstetrics for a while, but if you talked to the director of nursing…'

Ruth Stacey shook her head. 'I'm not taking you out of the theatre suite,' she said. '*That's* where you're needed. You know that scrub nurses with your experience aren't thick on the ground. Leave it with me. Something will come up in time.'

'Oh, I'm sure,' Annabelle said, obedient on the outside, rebellious within. 'Thanks for keeping it in mind.'

She appreciated that Ruth had other priorities, and didn't want to push the unit co-ordinator any harder than she already had.

So, change hospitals?

She thought about it as she left Ruth's office. Any other hospital in the city would add at least an hour to her daily commute between home and work and Mum's, but that might be worthwhile for the right timetable.

Although she knew it wasn't Ruth's fault, she hated being put on hold like this. A flat 'No, I can't change your shifts' might have been easier than this 'Be patient and I'll try to work something out for you' message she'd received on both her visits to the unit co-ordinator's office.

Out in the corridor a minute later, she was in no mood to meet Dylan. Both of them were on their way back to the theatre suite for another two or three hours of surgery.

What's Duncan doing right now? Annabelle wondered. Having an afternoon rest, as he's supposed to do? Or pestering the staff, disturbing the other children and trying to escape outside so he can run around? He needs me, and I don't want to be here!

'We've got another sportsman's knee coming up,' Dylan told her as they walked side by side towards the lifts. 'Should start a public awareness campaign. Warning—exercise can be dangerous to your joints.'

Annabelle could tell that the black humour was an

effort. He was feeling the same as she was. 'You don't want to be here today, do you, Dr Calford?' she said.

'Not much.'

'When are you going to talk to Jason Gregory?'

'Tomorrow morning, probably.'

'Tell me how it goes. If you want to,' she added quickly. 'If you need to offload. I mean, I saw that ruined knee, too.'

'Thanks,' he answered, but she had the feeling he had hardly heard.

In the end, Dylan told his sports-star patient the devastating news a little sooner than he'd planned. He needed to see another post-op patient in the two-bed room directly opposite Jason Gregory's private one, and heard the rugby player talking to his wife, Jan, as he crossed the corridor to Jason's room.

'Feels crummy.'

'Ask Sturgess if it's supposed to,' Jan replied.

'Wasn't Sturgess who operated. It was Calford. He's meant to be one of the best. He did Mark Allwood's knee last season, and he was playing again in about six weeks.'

'That's great!'

Yes, it was, Dylan agreed. But Mark Allwood's knee hadn't been anywhere near as bad as Jason's. He'd had a simple, low-grade synovial tear, easily dealt with through pinhole surgery.

Pausing in the doorway, he watched as Jason and his wife both turned to look at him. Their faces were expectant, nervous, hopeful. He took a deep breath.

'Let's have a talk about your surgery,' he said. 'If you're feeling up to it, that is.'

'Still a bit wonky,' Jason answered. 'But go on. Let's hear it. While Jan's here. She's better at coming up with the right questions than I am.'

'Like when will he be able to start training again?' Jan started at once. 'How much physio will he need? How much should it be hurting right now?'

'Let's start at the beginning,' Dylan said.

When he moved to the end of the bed and leaned on the high, wheeled meal tray, his back gave another spasm.

If this was me, hearing this sort of news about my future, how would I take it? he thought, and his stomach felt sick and leaden as he began to speak.

'What did Jason Gregory say?' Annabelle asked Dylan the next day, between operations.

'He's going to get a second opinion.'

'From who?'

'Alex, I expect.'

'Well, Alex is good. And experienced.'

'More so than me, obviously.'

'Yes. He's been doing it longer.'

There was a tiny silence, as if both of them felt uncomfortable about the intrusion of Alex's name into the conversation. Annabelle certainly did. It was like an old injury. You thought it had healed, then it flared up worse than ever after one small bump.

'Gregory's not suggesting you've overreacted to the problem, is he?' Annabelle asked finally.

Dylan looked tired and stressed. As if he hadn't slept, or was fighting off an infection. Somehow, though, the fatigue lines around his eyes and mouth took nothing away from his male appeal. Annabelle was as strongly caught up in it as she always seemed to be just lately.

The knowledge nagged at her—taunted her almost. It was as if some malign voice was whispering in her ear.

You were going to marry Alex, the voice said. Would that have made you safe from being so aware of another man? Could you ever have felt this way about Alex himself? When are you going to sort out what's real, what's important, what's fantasy and what's sheer desperation? When are you going to decide whether you're still furious with Dylan Calford, or whether you're going to give him the smug satisfaction of knowing that you're grateful because he was right?

'A mistake?' Dylan echoed. 'No, he and Jan are both being very good about it, actually. Sensible and cautious. Asking questions first and leaving decisions until later. Getting a second opinion is a perfectly valid thing to do at this stage.'

'But what will Alex tell them?'

'The same as I did, I should hope. And so would a specialist in Sydney or Melbourne, if they decided to go further afield.'

Annabelle took a deep breath. 'If that's the case, Dylan, why do you look so shattered?'

'It's obvious, isn't it? The man's career is over.' He sounded stiff and prickly and hostile…and something else. 'What exactly are you asking?'

'If you're OK, I suppose. That's all.'

'I'm fine,' he said abruptly, then walked away.

Dylan had told Annabelle that he was fine, and within a week it was true. The pain in his back eased gradually, until it wasn't there at all, and if he was taking things a little easier than usual, if he was more careful about the way he moved and avoided too much twisting, bending or lifting, then that was only sensible, wasn't it?

It wasn't that he was favouring his back, or that he was afraid.

He swam every day. Twice, when he could. It meant getting up earlier than usual, and plunging into a dark pool late at night when he didn't always feel like it, but if it strengthened his back muscles, then it was worth the effort. He knew of several nurses who'd had to change careers because of chronic back trouble, and he was going to take those cases, coupled with his own recent pain, as a well-timed warning.

Swimming twice a day helped him in one other critical area as well.

Annabelle.

It was the old, tried-and-true cold-shower principle.

Or something.

Work off the need. Go beyond desire, and into total exhaustion. Power through this simmering anger against Alex—thank goodness they'd managed to avoid each other to a large extent over the past couple of weeks—the way he powered through the water. A hundred lengths of his five-metre pool, morning and night. Each of the four major strokes. Bilateral breathing. Tumble turns at each end. By the time he stopped, the water was lapping the sides like storm waves, and his whole body was tingling.

It worked for his back, but he was kidding himself if he thought it did anything for the other stuff. The stuff with Annabelle. Eventually, something—or someone—was going to snap.

CHAPTER SIX

SOMEWHAT to Dylan's surprise, the prime candidate for a major meltdown turned out *not* to be Alex. The start of week six since the non-wedding signalled an abrupt change in the senior surgeon's mood.

Gone was the first week's flagrant bad temper and need to punish. Gone were the avoidance strategies which Dylan had, to be honest, welcomed with as much enthusiasm as Alex had put towards generating them.

Alex stopped scheduling private patients who lived on this side of the city for surgery at a private hospital on the other side of the city, forty minutes' drive away. He stopped delegating almost all the less critical cases to Dylan, and stopped discussing them only via terse phone conversations and abbreviation-laden e-mail messages.

He was breezy and witty during surgery, told a couple of risqué and not particularly good jokes— Annabelle's laugh didn't reach deeper than her tonsils—and remembered to ask Sharon about the birth of her niece.

But there was something about all of it that didn't feel right.

Or am I just a cynic? Dylan asked himself on Friday afternoon. They were doing another hip replacement—private patient, wife of a wealthy Brisbane businessman, the kind of case Alex always made a point of handling himself.

'Now,' he said to Annabelle, his tone affable and almost condescending, 'what kind of hip pack do you think I might be planning to use this afternoon?'

She wouldn't bite, just said in a pleasant, neutral way, 'We have both kinds available, Dr Sturgess. We've anticipated ceramic, but I haven't opened the pack.'

'Not eager to blow the hospital's budget today?'

'I'm never eager to do that.'

'No? Well, let's think, then.' He paused for a quarter of a second. 'Yes, I will use the ceramic hip.'

'Very good, Dr Sturgess.'

Sharon and Barb both glanced at her quickly, just as Dylan was doing. They all saw the way she closed her eyes and chewed on her lip, and they all saw Alex's little half-smile and heard him begin to whistle under his breath.

He drew unnecessary attention to Annabelle at least three more times during the procedure, and by the time it was finished, her cheeks were on fire and her well-washed top was clinging, damp and half-transparent, to her back. If Dylan hadn't known their history, he might almost—only it didn't quite ring true—have thought Alex was flirting with her.

'Annabelle, I'm glad I caught you.' She turned to find Ruth Stacey hurrying up behind her as she crossed the hospital foyer. 'Did you get my message?'

'Yes, I was going to phone your office when I got home.'

'And you're right, I'd still have been there!' the unit co-ordinator said wryly. 'I've got you the shifts you wanted, a regular four nights a week, eleven till seven, covering the weekend. It'll usually be Friday,

Saturday, Sunday and Monday, but occasionally we might have to juggle that a bit.'

'That's great,' Annabelle answered, relief washing over her like a cool breeze. 'When can I start?'

'Next roster goes out on Monday. You're down for two more weeks of days, and then you switch.'

'Thanks so much, Ruth! I really appreciate it.'

'I got the impression you needed it.'

'Oh, I do. Thanks.'

'Have a good weekend.'

'You, too, Ruth.'

Annabelle forgot, for the moment, how uncomfortable Alex had made her feel this afternoon. She floated out of the building on light feet, going through calculations she'd already made in her head at least a hundred times. Eleven-till-seven shifts, four times a week. She'd bring Mum over to stay for those nights. Duncan rarely woke in the night, so it wouldn't be too hard on Mum, and she'd be more than happy to do it. Then she'd be able to give Mum a good breakfast, make sure she took her medication and check her breathing, deliver her home and do her errands and her housework, albeit with Duncan's 'help'.

That would leave three nights a week for Annabelle to get a good sleep herself, plus whatever she could manage in the way of naps while Duncan watched television, or during the early hours of the night before work. She'd join a play-group with him, and maybe a kinder gym, and they'd go to story time at the library...

Outside the hospital's main entrance, the late February day was still bright and hot. To the left, there was a taxi rank and a bus stop, and straight ahead was a set-down zone where cars could park for a few minutes to pick up and let off passengers. To the right, a walkway led past the ambulance entrance and on to the staff car park just down the hill.

Annabelle was just about to head in that direction when she saw a familiar car in front of her. That was Alex's red open-top Mercedes sports, wasn't it? He hardly ever brought that car to the hospital. Normally, he drove his more anonymous and conservative dark green BMW.

Was it Alex's car? It wasn't him at the wheel. She checked the numberplate, which had his initials, followed by the number 007. Definitely, that was Alex's personalised plate, but in the driver's seat there was a woman whom Annabelle didn't know. She was silvery blonde, dressed to match the car, around forty years old, and absorbed in checking her face in a make-up mirror.

Short of openly staring, Annabelle couldn't observe anything more, but a second later she didn't have to. Behind her, as she began to walk on slow and rather numb legs towards the staff car park, she heard Alex's voice, speaking with loud, clear authority. Had he seen that she was just ahead of him? Yes, she was sure of it. That carrying voice was deliberately intended to capture her attention.

'Dylan, I'm not going to operate over the weekend,' he said. 'It's not necessary. Monday will be soon enough.'

'Medically, yes,' Dylan agreed. 'But in terms of the patient's best interests, I'm not so sure. We're talking about a young child and a couple of very anxious parents.'

'Monday,' Alex decreed. 'I'm going away. As you can see.'

'Alex, you're late,' came the woman's voice from the driver's seat of the car.

'Barely!'

'I've had some kind of security guard eyeing me with a black look on his face for the past fifteen minutes, darling.'

I have to sit down, Annabelle thought. *I should just keep walking but I don't know if my legs would get me as far as the car.*

Instinctively, she made a quick, clumsy turn, and headed for the left-most foyer door, but it was locked from the outside—the kind that had push-down bars on the inside and was intended only as an emergency exit. Turning again, she went some metres further along the walkway until she came to a low wall, edging a colourful garden bed, and sat down on that.

Rounding her shoulders and hugging her arms across her chest, she felt exposed and vulnerable and rubbery in her knees. The hot sun pressed on her back, and the light skirt and strappy blue top she'd changed into after finishing in the operating suite seemed inadequate.

Although she didn't look back the way she had come, the position turned out to be a box seat for hearing the scene that was still unfolding, and the cast of three—Dylan, Alex and the unknown blonde—delivered their lines perfectly.

'Ultimately, Alex, it's your call, of course,' Dylan was saying, just audibly.

'Yes, it is,' Alex answered much more loudly. 'And I've made it. We're operating on Monday.'

'If you keep talking shop like this, darling…' The blonde woman's voice carried naturally, without her having to try. 'I'll floor the lovely, responsive accelerator pedal of this gorgeous machine right now, and spend the weekend in Noosa very expensively by myself!'

'Never let a beautiful woman drive your best car, Dylan!' Alex quipped on a laugh. 'Stephanie, move over and give me the keys like a good girl.'

'Thought that would work!' she said, and Annabelle heard a clink as the keys changed hands.

The engine revved up, and they cruised off seconds later. Annabelle cast a quick look and saw Dylan shrug, turn and begin to walk in the direction of the same car park she herself had been heading for.

Only now did he catch sight of Annabelle. He stopped short. Too late, she pretended to be searching for something in her bag, then closed it quickly, got to her feet and said, 'Hi, Dylan!' in a voice so determined to remain steady that it came out more like a bark. 'Have a nice weekend,' she added on a squeak that was even worse, and began to hurry ahead of him towards the beckoning glimpse of her little car.

Please, don't follow me.

Her body language must surely say this to him, although she didn't stop to say it with words. Reaching her car, still shaking and weak-kneed, she took a covert look back the way she'd come, but didn't see him.

She felt sick, and would have leaned her forehead on the car roof if it hadn't been burning hot in the sun. Fumbling for her key, she couldn't get it into the lock because her hand was so tight and shaky. Instead, she just stood there, breathing in car fumes.

Alex, she was quite certain, had engineered that whole scene. Or if 'engineered' was too strong a word, he had at least set the wheels in motion, hoping it would happen. He knew Annabelle's schedule, and her habits, knew that it was highly likely she would be leaving through that exit at just after three on a Friday afternoon.

'Meet me at the front entrance at three, and we'll head off. Here are the keys to the Merc,' he must have said to the blonde. Stephanie. She had a name and a life and feelings, although she looked like she'd come direct from the local franchise of Rent-a-Mistress.

Alex didn't believe in renting when he could buy. He was from a wealthy Brisbane family, and he had connections. Stephanie might be the sister of an old school friend, back on the market after a divorce. Or she might be a regular on the charity circuit, a B-list celeb who could still wangle invitations to the right parties.

She would know about the healthy income that Alex pulled down each year, not just through his work but through his investments, and she would have jumped at him as soon as he'd made his move. She looked like exactly the kind of woman he'd always, and rather smugly, said to Annabelle that he didn't want for his wife—brittle hair and talon fingernails, collagen lips and a metallic laugh like someone sawing on a tin can, dollar signs in her eyes. 'So different to you, Annabelle.'

Future wife or long-term mistress or weekend lover, however, it didn't really matter. They were involved, and Alex had gone out of his way, in public, to make quite sure that Annabelle knew it.

I need to get into my car.

There was still no sign of Dylan, but somehow she was convinced he hadn't gone away. Other cars were leaving the car park, but she hadn't noticed his. She got her door open at last, and left it that way as she slid into the driver's seat. The car was like an oven, robbing her of breath once more.

Why does this feel so bad? she wondered.

She hadn't ever kidded herself that she was rapturously and naïvely in love with Alex Sturgess. On both sides, their decision to marry had been based on other feelings. She'd been aware of his faults, or so she'd thought, and more aware of them after he had walked out of their unfinished wedding. But to discover that he was prepared to punish her like this, over and above his pointed behaviour in surgery lately—it *hurt*!

A shadow fell across the interior of the car, and she looked up to find Dylan standing with his arm resting on the top of her open door. Behind him, she saw his car parked in one of the spots that had opened up as other nurses had ended their shifts and left.

'You were right, OK, Dylan?' she told him in a strained voice. 'You were right about Alex, from the moment you spoke up in the middle of the ceremony. And I understand the point of that meaningless marriage proposal of yours now. You were totally right. It would have been a disaster if Alex and I had gone through with the wedding. I was kidding myself that it would have worked, just because we'd been sensible about it and my family needed it. But that doesn't mean I'm feeling cheerful and happy and let off the hook, so do me a favour and don't—don't...' She stopped, unable to finish.

'I know,' he answered quietly. 'There's a kind of habit builds up, isn't there? A habit of care. You can't just switch it off, even if the other person endeavours to make it easy for you by behaving as badly as possible. It still hurts. It still changes the way you look at the world. And it still makes you wonder what you did to make it happen. Whether, somehow, it *is* your fault, only you can't see straight.'

'Thanks. Yes, that's how it is. Now, go away. I've admitted you were right, and I guess the reason you understand so well is because you've been through it, and I really feel for you about that, but—'

'That's not why I'm here.'

'No?'

'You shouldn't drive when you're feeling like this.'

'I'll be fine in a minute. Stop trying to look after me.' She aimed the key at the ignition.

'No, Annabelle.' His hand swooped down, but she saw it coming and closed her own fingers tightly around the keys. They ended up in three layers, like some odd piece of fruit, with a seed and flesh and skin. Her keys, wrapped in her fist, covered in his hand. The hand was warm, hard, sure of itself. She looked up, still rebellious, and found Dylan leaning over her with narrowed eyes and a steady, determined mouth.

Such a totally kissable mouth, she'd decided several weeks ago. Firm lips, not too full but not thin either. An illogical part of her instantly ached to find out how soft they would be, and how they would move. Demanding or gentle or wickedly seductive? A mix of all three?

Whichever way he kissed, she craved it, beyond her burning disappointment over Alex's behaviour, and knew that a man with Dylan's experience could hardly be in doubt as to how she felt.

'Let me have those keys right now, Belle,' he growled. It sounded like a proposition, not a threat.

Let me have the keys to your bedroom…the keys to your body…the keys to your soul.

'No. I'm fine,' she insisted.

For a moment, his grip tightened and he pulled even closer. She could see a faint mist of sweat in the tanned hollow of his throat, and she could smell the complex and satisfying fragrance of his skin, nutty and fresh.

His body was intimidating in a way that made her breathless and expectant. A huge part of her *wanted* him to take control, make decisions, crush her in his arms and kiss her so thoroughly that she didn't have time to think twice. Not about Alex or Dylan himself, her future, her family or anything else.

Except that it was impossible and wrong. She had to pick up Duncan and go over to Mum's. As she knew from experience, having Duncan with her was likely to make the household chores take twice as long, but her talk with Lauren at Gumnut Playcare recently had gone round and round in circles and hadn't thrown up any solutions.

Duncan had bitten Katie again. Katie's mother wasn't happy.

Understandably.

Duncan needed more attention and more freedom to be his active two-year-old self, but neither of these needs could be met in the structured environment of the child-care centre, without impinging unfairly on the other children. Annabelle no longer left him there for a second longer than absolutely necessary.

Abruptly, she twisted her arm, hoping to loosen Dylan's stubborn grip. She had expected resistance, but he didn't give it. Instead, she pulled her hand away easily, and looked up to find his eyes momentarily closed and his lower lip caught between his teeth as if he were fighting off a spasm of pain. Or was it something else?

'Dylan?' she blurted, her voice suddenly husky.

He opened his eyes, and straightened up. 'Can't stop you if you don't want to be stopped,' he said tightly.

It wasn't true. If he'd been prepared to use his body and his iron grip more forcefully, he could easily have won out.

'Yes, well,' she said awkwardly, then protested for the third time, 'I'll be fine.'

Only she wasn't.

There must have been a hold-up at the traffic lights on the main road just beyond the hospital driveway. Alex and Stephanie were only just coming past now. The attractive blonde was laughing, the lenses of her sunglasses flashing in the bright light. As he drove, Alex took his eyes from the road and shot a long, searching look across towards the car park where Annabelle sat.

Although she was facing the road, she would be hidden from his view behind the glare of her windscreen. Was he hoping to see if her car was still here? To check out the effect of his unpleasant game? What would he have done if their paths hadn't crossed outside the hospital doors as he'd hoped? Repeated the scene in a week's time? Or found another way to rub her nose publicly in his sexual success?

It was so petty, and yet it had worked. She felt exactly as he, no doubt, wanted her to feel.

A mess. As if this were her fault. Sullied and hunted and hurt.

Starting the engine, she reversed out of the space in a series of jerks, then turned the steering-wheel and cruised along the row of parked cars. The space at the end was empty. Turning left, she misjudged the distance, misjudged her speed and felt her hands slipping on the hot steering-wheel. Her left wheel rammed hard against the low concrete marker that edged the final space in the row, and there was a loud, violent sound.

She reversed again, as clumsily as before, then heard the sticky, rubbery noise of a rapidly deflating tyre wobbling over the asphalt.

Dylan appeared in her field of vision before she was out of the car. Annabelle leaned her elbow on the open window and yelled at him with a satisfying lack of control. 'If you say "I told you so," Dylan Calford, I'll reverse my car over your foot!'

'With the driving skill you're showing at the moment, I'm not worried,' he answered. 'You'd miss. Come on. Let's make a rational decision about what we're going to do.'

He strode closer, reached in and flicked up her lock, then opened the door and hauled her out, gripping her upper arm. Her breasts fetched up against the hard plane of his chest, and his mouth was close enough to kiss. Desire rocked her like an earthquake, making her gasp aloud. Their eyes met, and she saw his pupils start to dilate. No doubt—he was feeling this, too.

Then a car hooted, and he let her go. They were blocking the way, and so was her car.

'Got a spare?' Dylan asked.

'Yes.'

'And a jack?'

'Yes.'

'And both are in working order?'

'*Yes*, Dylan!'

'But you're still not.' His eyes narrowed again, and his gaze flicked up and down. 'This is what we'll do. And no arguments this time. I'll park your car and give you a lift back here later on. We'll change the tyre then. Right now, I'll run you wherever you need to go. I'm out of surgery for the day. Technically, I'm still on call, but Brian Collins is here, finishing off some stuff, and he'll cover for me if something comes up. He owes me for when I've done the same for him.'

'I'm not going straight home.'

'Didn't think you were.'

'I mean, even after I've picked up Duncan.'

'I didn't think you were,' he repeated steadily. 'To your mother's, right?'

He took her keys, and this time Annabelle didn't protest at all. Instead, she got lost in wondering how just that one light, brief and slightly ticklish touch, as he'd coaxed the keys from her hand, could have delivered such a jolt of pure, longed-for sensation. She stood there helplessly, watching him ease the crippled car into the empty space, then let him drop his arm around her shoulder.

If she'd turned just a little, if she'd leaned closer against him, she could have rested her head beside his neck and felt his cheek against her hair. He smelt so good. Like soap and coffee and eucalyptus. Comfortable and sexy at the same time.

'Come on,' he said. 'Sit with your eyes closed and make a mental shopping list while I drive.'

'It's not shopping today,' she answered. 'It's cleaning the kitchen and bathroom, changing a couple of light bulbs and paying some bills.'

'Your mother can't do the bills?'

'She gets flustered, and presses the wrong buttons.'

'Does she do them by that new automated phone system, with a credit card?'

'Yes. She was proud of herself originally for mastering it when they first introduced it, but she's been getting less capable lately. The breathlessness just wears her out, and she worries about the future for Duncan and me. She gets very anxious about all sorts of things. Silly things like keying in the right numbers when she's paying bills. Some days, she just goes to pieces about nothing at all.'

'Annabelle, did she push you to marry Alex?' Dylan asked quietly. He slid his arm away again as they reached his car.

'No.' Annabelle shook her head, then added reluctantly, 'She knew his mother, though. Always told me I could trust a man who was Lynette Sturgess's son.'

'I'm sure he wasn't involved with Stephanie before the wedding,' Dylan said, opening the passenger door for her.

'There are other ways to betray someone's trust. It's the pettiness of it that I hate, I think. Or the desire to punish. Oh, I don't want to talk about this any more!'

'Then we won't,' Dylan said simply, as he slid into the driver's seat and started the engine. 'If you want, we'll never talk about it again.'

*　　*　　*

'Let me do the light bulbs and the bills,' Dylan offered when they reached Helen Drew's building. Annabelle frowned at him and he said, 'Traditional man stuff. Less margin for error.'

She laughed. 'True! OK, I'll show you where the spare bulbs are, and I'll put Mum's credit card by the phone.'

She looked a lot better than she had half an hour ago. The sour taste no doubt left in her mouth by Alex's petty hurtfulness was slowly wearing off. Dylan understood how it felt. He'd been through the same thing with Sarah, but both the divorce and the property settlement were finalised now, and he could see it with a cooler perspective.

As Annabelle had suggested, the nastiness of it was degrading, somehow, to both parties, until the passage of time gave you some relief. He'd spent months wondering what it said about *him* that Sarah was so eager to go out of her way to exact various forms of petty revenge. She had been the one to leave their marriage. He was the one, surely, who should be seeking pay-back!

'You only care about your work,' she had accused him. 'You never have time for me.'

True. Of course it was. Partly. He'd warned her about that—about the fact that you paid a price for such a satisfying career and such a healthy income. And he'd done his best to compensate for it. Phone calls to her every time he had a break from surgery. Great holidays and getaways—expensive and luxurious and with no need for Sarah to lift a finger—whenever he had more than three days off in a row.

He had made the effort to take her out when he was way too tired to want to go. He'd even thought ahead to the distant possibility of kids. 'By then, I'll have my own specialist practice, and more control over my hours,' he'd told her. 'We'll be able to afford a housekeeper and a nanny, so that when I do have to put in long days, you won't be stranded at home with no help.'

Not enough, apparently, despite the fact that Sarah had always spoken so confidently about 'independence' and 'our own lives'. He had come home late one night when he'd been on call to find their town-house stripped of anything Sarah could claim as hers, and a note reading, 'It's over. You're never here, and I'm sick of it. Sarah.'

That at least had been honest, and necessary, if she'd felt that way.

But did she have to let him know exactly when, and in what circumstances, she'd first slept with the new lover she already had in tow? Did she have to 'accidentally' sell off his small but much-loved collection of old blues record albums at a garage sale for a fraction of what they were worth?

If there was that much bitterness stored up, couldn't she have expressed it earlier, in a way that would have let him at least *try* to take some action?

It was only over the past few months that he'd learned to see all of this as her problem, rather than a reflection on himself. He felt freer now. And he understood Annabelle's current feelings better than she could know.

Meeting her mother, he was a little self-conscious, remembering the circumstances of their first encounter. But all Helen Drew said, in her wheezy voice, was, 'Thank you for driving my daughter here.' She offered him a drink, but he declined. Playing things cautiously.

'The new light bulbs are in the laundry cupboard,' Annabelle told him. 'The one in the bathroom has gone, one in the bedroom and one in the hall.'

'Won't take long,' he said. 'Then I'll take care of the bills.'

'I'll be in the kitchen,' she answered. 'Duncan and Mum are going to read some stories on the balcony.'

It took Dylan five minutes to do the light bulbs, and then he keyed in the pay-by-phone number for the first of Helen's bills. He understood how she could get flustered with this. He'd once calculated that he needed to press over fifty digits to pay his electricity bill—still cheaper and easier than writing and mailing a cheque, however, and he had it down to a fine art now.

Such a fine art, in fact, that he automatically began keying in his own credit-card number instead of Helen's, since hers was with the same company and the first four digits of both cards were the same.

'Damn!' he muttered, then finished the number and waited for the recorded voice to repeat it back to him, ask if it was correct and offer him the opportunity to try again if it wasn't.

Strange that your whole perspective could change in the space of a few seconds, while listening to the meaningful phrase, 'If yes, press 1.'

If yes, press 1.

'Yes' would make things easier for Annabelle and her mother by saving them hundreds of dollars on utility bills which Dylan himself could easily afford. Eventually, when Helen's credit-card bill arrived— assuming she checked it carefully enough—she would realise that the payment hadn't gone through on her card.

'Yes' wasn't just about money, though. In fact, as far as he was concerned, it wasn't about money at all. He knew that Annabelle Drew was a woman he had to take seriously. 'Yes' amounted to a clear and deliberate decision on his part to do exactly that.

His index finger hovered over both digits for a second longer.

If 'Yes' press 1, to re-enter press 2.

When his fingertip touched the 1 button, and the electronic beep sounded in his ear, he suddenly felt very, very good.

Moments later, a voice told him brightly, 'Payment has been accepted.' He scribbled the date and the electronic receipt number on the bill. He dealt with two more bills in the same way, using his own card each time, then saw that Helen and Duncan were still reading on the balcony and went in search of Annabelle.

She was wearing pink rubber gloves, and was squirting an abrasive cream cleanser onto the stove top.

'All done,' he told her, coming across to lean against the adjacent stainless-steel sink. 'Could I take Duncan to the playground, or something?'

'That would be great,' she answered. 'Any second, he's going to get sick of reading and want to ''help'', and we'll be here forever.'

'Forever sounds good,' Dylan said, then leaned his body and tilted his face, met her slightly—but not very—surprised look in his direction, and kissed her.

CHAPTER SEVEN

ANNABELLE didn't hesitate, or push away. She kissed Dylan back.

Wrapping her arms around his neck and keeping the gloved parts out of the way, she stepped closer so that they were hard against each other. She drank the taste of his mouth like wine, with eager, parted lips. She closed her eyes.

It felt so good. So right. As if it should have happened days ago, and, at the same time, as if now was the perfect moment.

Dylan spread his hands and ran them across her ribs, then up to her breasts. He took their weight and lifted them, searing his thumbs across her hardened nipples. She felt his fingers whisper just above the neckline of her top, then climb to stroke the loose hair back from her hot neck.

She had to stretch up on tiptoe to hold him without getting the wet gloves on the back of his shirt, and she teetered. It was a very satisfying form of unsteadiness, with his solid support against her. He whispered hotly in her ear, 'I've got you.'

'I know.'

'Not letting you go.'

'Don't. Please.' She printed kiss after kiss on his mouth—kisses that were hot and hungry and eager for more. His response swept her away. His kisses were imperious, confident, teasing and meltingly sweet.

'Hold me, Annabelle,' he said fiercely against her mouth. 'I want to feel you.'

'I can't. The gloves…'

'Doesn't matter.' He gathered her more tightly against him, driving the breath high into her lungs. She felt giddy. Just wanted to laugh and cry and kiss him for hours.

'Mummy! Clean a baffroom now?'

She heard Duncan's running feet on the carpet, and Mum's smoke-darkened voice, still on the balcony. 'One more story, Dunc?'

'No. Help clean a baffroom now.'

Annabelle pulled away from Dylan, her breathing still fast and high. Dylan turned to face the sink and grabbed a sponge. There were wet splodges on the back of his shirt.

'I've dripped cleaning stuff on you,' she said.

'I told you, it doesn't matter.'

Duncan arrived, oblivious to the struggle going on in both of them and to the nuances beyond their trivial words. 'I need a sponge,' he announced.

He loved helping to clean the bathroom, because it was such a lovely messy job, and the more enthusiasm he displayed, the messier it was.

'Take him for a walk?' Dylan suggested. 'I'd like to.'

But Duncan was stubborn, and wouldn't go. He was going to help clean that bathroom or collapse in a screaming heap, and that was that.

'I'm not going to push it,' Annabelle told Dylan quietly.

Mum had also arrived in the kitchen now, and she nodded. 'Best not.'

'I'd win eventually—I'm bigger than you,

Duncan!' Annabelle went on. 'But the price is pretty high, late on a Friday afternoon. Can't send him with you, Dylan, if he doesn't want to go, since he doesn't know you that well.'

They got the cleaning done eventually, with Mum in the background berating herself for being so useless.

'Now, about dinner,' Annabelle said to her finally.

'Don't worry. I've still got a couple of those lovely leftover take-away meals you brought me a few weeks ago. I'll thaw one out in the microwave.'

When Annabelle finally reached Dylan's car—Duncan still had a streak of dried cleanser running down his arm—she only wanted one thing. Dylan Calford, holding her in his arms and kissing her silly.

'We have to go back and fix the tyre so I can drive my car. After that, are you…coming back to my place?' she asked him. Didn't even try to pretend it was a casual suggestion.

He glanced across at her, and her heart caught in her throat at the look in his eyes. 'Am I invited?'

'Yes. You are.'

It was still fairly early when they got home. Dylan had followed her all the way from the hospital. Because he was still unsure of the best route, or to check that she was driving safely? After they'd changed the flat tyre, he had commented on a strange noise her engine was making. At the moment, she didn't care about either the noise or Dylan's motivations.

Duncan wanted a swim. 'I'll take him,' Dylan offered. 'I've got a pair of board shorts in the back of my car this time.'

'Want to go in the pool with Dylan, Dunc?'

He nodded energetically, which surprised Annabelle a little. He didn't always take to other people straight away.

While they were swimming, she tossed some salad, heated garlic bread in the oven and made a quick pesto out of a big bunch of mint leaves from the garden, crushed walnuts, parmesan cheese and olive oil. The three of them ate beside the pool at the rickety white plastic table and chairs which Annabelle was desperate to replace but couldn't afford to.

That didn't seem so important any more. There was a satisfaction in knowing that everything around her was her own, and that she was finding ways to manage without the effortless luxury of Alex's wealth.

Alex had never spent more than a few minutes at her house. 'Best if we go to my place.' But that wasn't always true. It wasn't 'best' every single time, even if Alex's pool was twice as big, and his house was cooler, his fridge had more drinks in it and his housekeeper would clean up after them. Eventually, always going to his place created an imbalance.

Dylan doesn't seem to mind coming here, she thought.

By the time they'd finished eating, Duncan was ready for bed. 'Quick as we can tonight,' she promised Dylan.

'I'll still be here when you get back,' he said.

'I hoped you would be,' she answered, a little shyly.

He was still wearing only the pair of baggy, colourful board shorts he'd put on to swim with Duncan, and she had to fight to keep her gaze from lingering on the muscular contours of his tanned shoulders and chest. He seemed casual about it, not showing off.

Too distracted by her own body, perhaps. She recognised the way he was watching her, eyes softly alight, and it made her feel alive, expectant, more sensual than usual. She wasn't used to the feeling, but she liked it.

'Thank you, Duncan, sweetheart,' she whispered to her little boy, when he drifted off to sleep before she'd even finished his story. 'This was a good night for getting sleepy early.'

She kissed his smooth little forehead, brushed back some sweat-dampened tendrils of hair, adjusted the position of the cooling fan that played over him while he slept, and went out to Dylan by the pool.

She went straight into his arms.

'Hello,' he said. He brushed his mouth across hers. 'Nice surprise.' His arms tightened around her.

'Is it?' She looked up into his face, so close to hers. 'Nice, I know, but a surprise?'

'You came right up to me. Didn't break your stride. You held out your arms.' His mouth was a fraction of an inch from hers now as he spoke. 'It was great. I wanted you to do that, but I didn't think you would.'

'Why not, Dylan?'

He smiled. 'Things never happen exactly the way you want them to. I've been having this great scenario playing in my head about standing like this with you in the pool, and slowly peeling your swimsuit from your body.'

'And why can't that happen?'

'Because I'm slowly going to peel your clothes off right here instead.'

'Gee, I walked right into that one, didn't I?'

He just laughed, and began to slide the straps of her top off her shoulders. Annabelle closed her eyes and let it happen. His touch made her throb and pulse all over. At first, she was so overwhelmed by sensation that she couldn't move, but when he slid her top down to her waist, unfastened her skirt and dragged both garments down over her hips, she suddenly wanted to share in his exploration.

How did he feel? Was his skin as hot and sensitive as hers? Or was it still cool and satiny from his earlier swim? How would he react when she touched him? Would he—?

Ah, yes! She felt a delicious sense of power as he groaned. Letting her eyelids flutter open for a few seconds, she saw that his eyes were closed and his head was thrown back. He was dragging his teeth across his bottom lip, as if he'd reached a point where pleasure almost became pain.

Wanting to soothe him, she left his board shorts hanging on his hips, low and precariously positioned, cupped her hands around his jaw and kissed him with soft, tender lips. She loved his hungry response.

Thirty seconds later, they lost their balance, made it worse by clinging to each other too hard and crashed into the pool, still locked in each other's arms. Both of them came up laughing.

'Did you do that on purpose?' he asked.

'No. But I'm glad it happened. It's lovely.'

The water felt good, so milky mild in this temperature that there was no shock, just an invigorating freshness. They stood up together, and he brushed the hair back from her face then reached around and unclipped her bra. 'Don't need this. Or these…'

Her top and skirt were still bunched across her hips.

He slid them down and she wriggled, helping him. His board shorts had lost their last tenuous hold on his hips as they'd hit the water. He kicked his way out of them, then curled himself low in the water to remove her own clothing.

The sight of his wet, dark head so close to her upper thighs made something twist deep inside her. She sank back in the water, floating on her back, and shook skirt and top and underwear off her feet. Dylan scooped his arms beneath her and held her against him, looking deep into her eyes.

'So…' he said.

'So…' she echoed.

'Funny, the way things turn out!'

'Mmm.'

Funny, and a little frightening. She could feel him pressed against her in graphic detail. One full breast was cushioned against his chest, and the other nudged his cupped hand as he held her. Her hip was pressed into his stomach, very low down…

She had slept with Alex, but not until their relationship had already been established and serious, running along in a groove which both of them had already recognised was heading to marriage.

Alex had always been courteous about it, softening her up with a lavish meal and wine, compliments and attention, as if he had to coax her into it, as if they only made love because of his needs, never hers. It seemed incredible to her now that she'd actually responded to that. She'd liked it. Why? Alex had been right. It *had* been about his needs. She'd never felt any urgency of desire for him. Was that why she'd responded to his courteous approach?

With Dylan, it was different. Desire was pulling on

her. Desire was telling her to ignore the fact that they didn't really have a relationship at all. That didn't seem important at the moment. In fact, she preferred it this way.

There was no sense of appropriate transactions taking place, the way there had been with Alex. Dinner in exchange for love-making. Marriage in exchange for her good name and breeding. Security in exchange for wifely support and the creation of heirs. Despite all the problems Alex's proposal had promised to solve, at some deeper level their relationship had hedged her in.

Now she felt free.

Wild, too, in a way she'd never let herself feel before. Vic had always been the wild one. Annabelle had felt constrained to be the opposite—the one who'd given support to Mum, the one who'd pleased Dad by working hard towards a good career, the one who'd set an example in the hope of reining her sister in.

There was no one for whom to set an example tonight, no transactions laid out on the table. There was just her and Dylan, a sultry night and the caress of the water.

Funny, the way things turned out.

Suddenly, she wasn't frightened any more at all. She wanted it, and she wanted it to be like this— open-ended, non-contractual and, above all, *physical*.

'You're beautiful, Annabelle,' Dylan said softly. His black eyes glinted and danced with reflected light from the surface of the pool.

'I'm not,' she answered automatically. 'I—'

'Don't argue. Don't. You're beautiful. Don't know whether to stand here kissing every inch of your wet skin for another hour or whether to take you to bed right now. Help me decide. We're going to bed, right?'

'If we weren't, I wouldn't have let you—'

'Didn't think so.' He smiled. 'Appreciate that about you. No games. I hate games.'

'Then take me to bed now, Dylan.'

He carried her as far as the grass just beyond the pool gate, then set her on her feet and reached for the towel hung over the pool fence. Annabelle didn't want to lose his touch, not for a second. She pulled on his hips, feeling the swift, satisfying brush of his arousal across her stomach. He shuddered and his arm came around her back, anchoring her wet breasts and chill-hardened nipples against his chest.

With the towel left dangling in one hand, he kissed her—kissed her mouth and her neck, her throat and her breasts. They stood entwined together like that for a long time, cool and wet and naked, lost in the taste and feel of each other. When finally he dragged his mouth from hers and wrapped the towel around them both, she was almost dry, and so was he.

'What was this towel for? I've forgotten,' he said.

'To make love on, I presumed,' she teased. 'Like a picnic blanket.'

He didn't answer, but his grin was wicked, and the glint in his dark eyes was even wickeder. One flick of his outstretched arms laid the big, fluffy towel on the grass.

Annabelle gasped. 'Dylan, I didn't mean it.'

'Too bad. You shouldn't say things you don't mean to a man in my condition. A man, what's more, who was anticipating this eagerly enough to think of protection.' Annabelle heard the crackle of a small packet in his hand.

'The neighbours—' she protested.

'Won't see a thing. It's dark.'

He touched her teasingly, his hands light and seductive. Annabelle knew he must have felt the way she shuddered, the way she moulded herself against him and responded.

'Do you mind that I was thinking ahead?' he asked.

'I was, too. But I hadn't…come up with anything. So, no, I don't mind.'

'Good…' She hardly realised what he was doing until he had her on the ground, pinned beneath him and looking up into his grinning face.

He traced the tip of his finger over her lips, along her jaw, down her throat and between her breasts, then he cupped her—so lightly that his touch felt like the brush of some silky fabric.

'Decision time, Annabelle,' he said softly. 'Do you want to go inside?'

'No…'

'Good,' he said again, then propped himself up on his elbows, on either side of her ribs. 'Because neither do I.'

Wild. It was wild. A fever of hands and mouths, pressure and rhythm that caught Annabelle up in a tornado of sensation and didn't let her go until both of them had reached a passionate release. In its aftermath, she lay there on the rumpled towel still throbbing, hot and swollen, clinging to him as if he were her life-raft in a huge black ocean.

She felt shaken by the realisation of how close she'd come to never knowing that a man and a woman could come together this powerfully. The chemistry between herself and Alex had been wrong, and she'd never realised it. Couldn't have realised it until she'd experienced a chemistry that was right.

Suddenly, she felt sorry for the other man. All his wealth and professional success, his sense of control and of his own importance—that fatal combination of character traits which had encouraged him to select her as his future wife and then turn on her the moment he felt she'd let him down. All of that added up to so little that was truly important.

And had Vic, after all, with her flamboyant and headlong dance through life, discovered an essence that Annabelle had overlooked?

After a long interval of lying still, entwined together and saying nothing, Dylan picked up her hand and pressed his lips to her knuckles one by one, and then to each fingertip.

'What are you thinking, Belle? I can hear something ticking in there.' He knocked lightly on her forehead, then turned it into a caress.

'That maybe I'm starting to understand my sister better than I once did.'

'Yeah? Tell me.'

'Only because— I mean— Gosh! Can't explain!'

'Try,' he invited.

'Oh, OK. Um, OK.'

But she was distracted. The unaccustomed heaviness of sated senses felt too good, and when Dylan stretched out his fingers to brush them across her nipples, she was mesmerised by the sight, and by her own response.

She tried again. 'I'm just…thinking about things I've missed out on that Vic instinctively knew.'

'Like what?'

'Oh, being a little selfish occasionally. Responding to what feels good. Not asking too many questions.' She said a bit more, then stopped, wondering if any of it had even made sense, let alone been worth his attention. 'I'm sorry,' she finished.

'You're allowed to talk about her. About anything. Just because my hands like to wander, it doesn't mean my attention is.'

'Maybe it's *my* attention that's wandering.'

'Where's it going?'

'Inside. To somewhere a little more comfortable.'

'Sounds good.'

And it *was* good. It was fabulous, all over again. They fell asleep on her bed, tangled in each other's arms, and Annabelle didn't awaken until the early hours—the darkest hours—when she was jolted from sleep by the sound of glass shattering in her bathroom.

For several seconds, she was disoriented and panicky. Who was there? What were they doing? Where was Duncan? Safe? Her heart was pounding in her ears, and she covered the distance from deep sleep to high alert far too fast. Then she heard Dylan's voice, swearing.

'What happened?' she called.

But he didn't hear.

She rolled clumsily out of bed, still naked and feeling suddenly vulnerable. There was no clothing handy to put on, unless she opened a drawer or wardrobe and scrabbled around in the dark for a T-shirt or a dress.

Heading for the bedroom door, she croaked, 'Dylan?'

'I knocked over a bottle of cough medicine and it broke,' he called. 'I'm sorry. It's a real mess.'

'That's OK, as long as you didn't cut yourself.'

She reached the bathroom, just outside her bedroom and to the left, and at that moment he turned on the light. It blinded and disoriented her afresh, and Dylan had his hand shading his eyes, too.

'I shouldn't have been fumbling around in the dark,' he said. 'Should have turned this on straight away. But I didn't know if the light would wake Duncan up.'

'It wouldn't have. And apparently the breaking glass hasn't either.'

She grabbed a towel, wrapped it around her body and tucked the end down in front, between her breasts. As a covering, it was both uncomfortable and inadequate, and if Duncan did awaken and she had to cuddle him, it would be bound to work loose. Tiptoeing along to his room, however, she saw him still fast asleep.

Back in the bathroom, she found Dylan picking pieces of lethally sharp brown glass out of the puddle of sticky pink syrup that was still spreading wider beside the basin and threatening to drip onto the floor. The mirrored medicine cabinet above the basin gaped open, and several of the bottles and packets were out of place.

'Got somewhere to put this?' Dylan asked, holding out the handful of sticky glass slivers he'd collected.

'Here.' She grabbed one of Duncan's plastic pouring cups from the side of the tub and gave it to him.

'When I've got all the big pieces, we can wash the rest down the sink.'

'What were you looking for in the cabinet?'

'Painkillers.'

'You've got a headache?'

'Uh…yes.' He nodded. Then he frowned.

'I haven't got anything very strong.'

'Just to take the edge off.' He controlled a sigh. 'I should head home, too.'

'Because of the headache?'

'No, because of Duncan.'

'Oh, right.'

'Best, isn't it?'

'I hadn't, um, thought that far ahead. But, yes. You're right. It's best.'

He stopped fishing for bits of glass and looked at her. Looked at her, actually, for the first time since she'd stumbled into the bathroom, blinded by the sudden light. He smiled, too. 'That doesn't mean I can't come back again another night. Quite soon, I'm hoping.'

She relaxed, and wasn't sure why she'd been tense in the first place. Just the shock of thinking for several seconds that she had a violent stranger smashing glass in her bathroom at three in the morning?

'I'm hoping it's soon, too,' she said. 'And I'm sorry about your…your headache.'

Because why would Dylan say he had a headache if he didn't?

'Annabelle, I'm a little bit worried.'

'Yes, Mum?'

'I'm probably just being silly.'

'I'm sure you're not. Tell me.'

'Well, I just got my credit-card statement, and none of this quarter's bills are on it, and it seems as if they should have—' She broke off to cough, and

Annabelle waited. She was standing in the hospital's main foyer, from where she often phoned Mum during her lunch-break. 'Except that I haven't received any reminder notices,' her mother continued. 'But what if they cut off the phone?'

'Let's not worry about that yet,' Annabelle soothed. The phone obviously hadn't been cut off yet, since Mum had phoned from her unit. 'I'm coming over straight after work, after I've picked up Duncan, but we'll be later than usual, because we'll have to get the bus. The garage said the car won't be ready until five.'

'All right.'

The car engine's recent strange noise had turned into an urgent need for replacement parts which Annabelle knew was going to cost hundreds. She'd taken it back to Dylan's car mechanic, since the location was convenient and they'd charged a little less than she'd expected last time.

No more child-care fees after this week, and there's still some room on the credit card...

'But I gave Dr Calford my credit card,' Mum was saying. 'Could he have made a mistake and—? But, no,' she interrupted herself. 'That seems impossible. I just can't understand why nothing's appeared on the statement.'

'I'm sure there's an explanation. Mum, I have to go and get ready for the afternoon list. Just don't even think about it until I get there, OK? I'm sure it'll be something to do with the issue date of the statement, that's all.'

It had only been ten days since the bills had been paid. Dylan wasn't operating today. He'd had a seminar to attend in the morning, and a fracture clinic in the afternoon. They'd seen each other on the weekend, and they were seeing each other tonight, and Annabelle was hugging the whole thing to herself like a big box of chocolates that she wasn't planning to share.

Happy about it. Happy about him. Happiest because she wasn't thinking beyond now, tonight or this week. She was just letting it happen—something she'd never done before in her life. When she got back to the nurses' changing room, there was a note from Dylan in her locker.

'Dropped in but missed you,' he'd written, in his confident doctor's scrawl. 'Was hoping we could grab lunch before my clinic, but Barb mentioned you were running some errands. See you tonight. Dylan.'

The afternoon's list was uneventful, the bus was on time at five past three and Annabelle picked Duncan up just fifteen minutes later than usual. This was his last week at Gumnut Playcare, and every time she saw the way his face changed from glowering frustration to sparkling happiness when she arrived there, she was thankful about it. Today, as icing on the cake, there was another 'incident note' in his pocket. He'd hit Ryan over the head twice with a block.

At Mum's, after another bus ride, he was difficult for much of the time. Wouldn't stop jumping on the couch and running around and around the living room. When Annabelle got angry with him, he got angry back, and shouted a word he certainly hadn't learned in her company.

She ignored it completely, but knew that her voice was tear-filled as she said, 'What am I going to do with him, Mum?'

'He's two, love, and he's active and hungry for life.

If he was growing up on a farm, he'd be fine. You're doing everything right, and we both know he has a loving little heart underneath.'

'Next week...'

'I'm still worried it's going to be too much for you.'

'It's not forever. Just until he settles down. When he starts school, I hope. And I'm worried it's going to be too much for *you*!'

'Nonsense!' Brave words, fragile tone. Then Mum coughed and struggled for breath, needed her oxygen, but was determined to give Annabelle the credit-card statement to look at first.

'Are the bills filed away, Mum?' she asked, when things had settled down a little.

A *little*. Duncan was still jumping on the couch. Annabelle decided to let him do it, this once. Some kids, apparently, never even *thought* of jumping on couches. What would that be like? she wondered.

'No, I got them out again,' Mum said.

'It does seem as if the payments should have appeared on this statement. Let me get their transaction numbers and phone the enquiry lines, see if there's been some kind of a glitch.'

A couple of frustrating phone calls reassured both of them that no phone line or electricity service was about to be disconnected. Everything was in order. The bills had apparently been paid by magic.

No, Annabelle understood finally. It had taken her way longer than it should have done.

Not by magic. By Dylan.

It didn't click until she and Duncan arrived at Dylan's garage to pick up the car.

'So how much will it be?' she made herself ask brightly, dreading the answer.

'Four hundred and ninety-five dollars,' the head mechanic said, then gave her a leering stare. 'Isn't your doctor boyfriend going to pick up the tab for you this time?'

'What did you expect me to say?' Annabelle asked Dylan angrily, an hour later.

'Not much. A small thank-you, maybe.' He looked wary, a little distant, and he was watching her carefully.

He had only arrived at her place a minute ago—with another huge assortment of take-away containers, even though she had already told him she would cook—and she'd launched into her angry interrogation straight away, while Duncan was still safely running around in the back garden.

Had Dylan put those bills of Mum's on his own card?

Yes.

And was he intending to pick up all or part of the tab at her garage, as he'd apparently done before?

Yes to that, too.

Why?

That was obvious, wasn't it?

She paced the kitchen, got distracted for a moment by the sight of him unpacking the twelve…no, fourteen…plastic containers, all of them steaming with hot food, and demanded, 'What am I supposed to do with all that?'

'Eat the dishes we fancy tonight, and freeze the rest.'

'No. You can take it home. I hate this. Why have you started doing this?'

'What's "this"?'

'You know!'

'Helping—'

'No! You were the one who made me see what a horrible, mercenary kind of transaction was going on between Alex and me, and now you're doing the same thing.'

'Annabelle—'

'I'm not your mistress, Dylan. The garage man made it quite clear he thought you were paying for favours received. And I'm not your charity case. I don't want to *need* you. I just want...'

To want you. She didn't quite dare to say it, since the wanting was so strong.

'You don't have to pay for me, or find ways to elevate my lifestyle to your level,' she went on. 'If my lifestyle isn't good enough for you, then *I'm* not good enough for you. And if any part of what's going on here is because you feel sorry for me, you can get out of my house right now.'

'Since none of that applies, I'll stay put,' he answered lightly.

The lightness angered her further. He wasn't taking this seriously. He wasn't taking *her* seriously! Maybe the wanting was only this strong on her side.

'Don't belittle my feelings,' she said. 'This is important.'

'I'm not belittling your feelings. I'm belittling what I did. I paid a few bills for your mother, and set up an arrangement at my garage.'

'Yes, Alex was very willing to take on my family and financial obligations, too. I was happy about that until I realised—until *you* made me see—what he expected in return—a porcelain wife with a saintly aura so extreme it could be permanently damaged, in his eyes, by your outrageous behaviour at our wedding.'

'Hey!' Dylan growled. 'You know I never meant that comment of mine to carry the way it did! Haven't we dealt with that? It's behind us. And as for comparing me with Alex, saintliness is the last thing on my mind when I think of you, Annabelle.'

She ignored the suggestive, caressing lilt in his voice and stood her ground. 'I'm not going to be *kept*. Or helped. I don't want to be dependent on the man I'm…' She hesitated, and searched for the right word. 'The man I'm sleeping with.'

'What if I'm not prepared to build a relationship on those terms?' he shot back at her immediately. 'What if I believe that there's always give and take? That you can't even have a casual fling without need and support going both ways? And anyway, as far as I'm concerned, this isn't—'

She ploughed over him. 'It's not going both ways, the way you've engineered it. It can't go both ways. I've got nothing to give.'

He ignored her.

'I'm not backing down on this, Annabelle. What you're saying is impractical and artificial. You're the one dealing in transactions.'

'Am I? If that's true, then I guess it's over. It is over, Dylan. It has to be.'

She could hardly believe she'd said it. The words had flashed out of her mouth like a knife blade flashing out of its sheath. As soon as they'd been spoken, they settled into place as if they were puzzle pieces.

They fitted. She didn't particularly want them to, but they did.

'It has to be,' she repeated tightly.

She had started this too soon. She had too many issues trailing in her wake. Feelings, obligations, questions. It was very nice to have a man like Dylan in her life—a man who set her on fire, and bossed her around a little bit, with a wicked gleam in his eyes. But she wasn't ready, and she desperately didn't want to fall into the same pattern she'd had with Alex. She didn't trust Dylan's confidence on the issue, didn't trust his belief that he was too different from the senior surgeon to let it happen.

'Oh, for heaven's sake!' Dylan crossed the kitchen in three strides, and pulled her into his arms. His confidence didn't appear to flag.

And maybe he was right to be confident, because she didn't fight him off, just looked helplessly up into his face, melting at his touch the way she always did.

'You don't mean this,' he said.

'I—I do, actually.'

'What, you're turning it off, just like that? One minute we're on fire for each other…' He gave her a graphic verbal sketch about exactly what this had meant to them over the past ten days. Secret heat in the way they looked at each other. An almost painful anticipation about being together. Feverish couplings in her bedroom…and other places. 'The next minute,' he went on, 'you're telling me you've switched off the current. I don't believe it. You still feel it. You *do*!'

The way he was touching her, and the way she responded, proved his point, but she at last managed to flatten her hand against his chest and push him away. At the same time, Annabelle had to bite on her lower lip to stop herself from letting her mouth drift open to receive his kiss.

'That's not the thing that counts for me,' she said. 'I just don't like…the other places where this is going. You shouldn't have paid those bills, or made the arrangement with your mechanic. Not without asking.'

'If I'd asked, would you have let me?'

'No.'

'There you are!'

'*No!* Tricking me into accepting help is worse. I can't explain why this is so important. I'm obviously not explaining. Not well enough. But it is.'

He tried to argue some more, but she resisted. It was painful. Almost impossible. But she managed it, and finally she saw an angry acceptance cloud his eyes.

'You're almost as stubborn as Alex, do you know that?' he muttered.

'Good! It's right to be stubborn sometimes.'

He controlled a sigh. 'I'd better go, then, hadn't I?'

'Yes, I—I think so. Please, take…' Her gesture towards the hot containers on the counter-top died in the face of his laughter.

'Some of the food?' he finished for her. 'Hell, don't be so petty, Annabelle! There's a big picture out there, you know. You're not seeing it, and I can't force you to. So let's leave it at that. I'll see you, OK? Sorry we didn't get a little further than this.'

She mumbled some inept agreement and followed him to her front door. Then Duncan called out for her and she hurried out to the garden, wondering if there was any way she and Dylan could have handled this without making such a mess of it.

CHAPTER EIGHT

THE pain was back.

It came on so gradually that Dylan thought his mind was playing tricks at first. This new hot spot low in his spine wasn't related in any way to the pain he'd had before. Thinking about that first night at Annabelle's, he concluded that making love on a towel on the grass hadn't been such an erotic and inspired idea after all. He'd got a bruise on his spine, or something, from the hard ground beneath them.

Smashing her bottle of cough syrup seemed like proof that he shouldn't be seeking to mask the issue with medication. He left the painkillers alone for the next week or more, and listened helplessly to his nerve-endings telling him, It's getting worse. It's more than a bruise.

Still, he made excuses. A lot of doctors were good at that when it came to their own bodies. Too much swimming, he decided. And the seat-back in his car wasn't positioned correctly. He'd had a couple of difficult operations. He was stressed. All sorts of plausible things.

He definitely felt stressed after Annabelle's meltdown on Tuesday night. He understood what she was saying, but felt that she was coming at the whole thing from the wrong angle. Would have tried to talk to her about it some more, only he didn't know how to say it. There were some missing links in his own understanding as well.

He was sure, though, that her comparing him to Alex was hugely and almost sinfully unfair. So perhaps he'd had a fortunate escape from more tangled perceptions further down the line. Perhaps his experience with Sarah wasn't far enough in the past, after all. At least Sarah had had a single, specific complaint. 'You're never here.'

Some people, on the other hand, had a knack for creating problems in a relationship where none truly existed. If Annabelle was one of them...

And meanwhile, there was the pain in his back.

It started waking him in the night, and he skulked off to a physiotherapist who had a practice at the shopping centre near where he lived. He'd never heard of her. She wasn't on the list of people to whom he or Alex referred their own patients when necessary.

This, of course, was the whole point of seeing her. He didn't want this getting back to anyone else in the profession.

She seemed perfectly competent and pleasant, and had all the right qualifications. He sketched out the problem. She said it was very common, and gave him some ultrasound massage and some exercises. One of the mentholated heat ointments might help, too, she said. He picked some up at the chemist immediately, and slathered it on as soon as he got home.

If it helped, it didn't help much.

He started to notice the pain in surgery again, worse than that first bout after the sailing trip, and thought rebelliously, Why? There's no family history. His parents, in the United States, still maintained an active lifestyle, and his older sister, who also lived there, had never had any back problems that he knew about, even during her two pregnancies.

In addition, his posture was good. He did do a certain amount of lifting and pulling in his profession, but not enough to generate a chronic problem, or so he would have thought.

It had to be the sailing. He'd pulled a muscle or bruised a vertebra without realising it, and he kept unconsciously aggravating the injury before it had fully healed. He just needed to take things easy, do the exercises, get some more massage and be careful.

All this good sense...and none of it worked.

Duncan left Gumnut Playcare for the last time without a backward glance. Each of the staff gave him a hug, raised their voices a little too high to be natural and said they hoped he'd come back for *lots* of visits. Duncan scowled, turned and ran for the car.

I'm going to make the night shifts work! Annabelle vowed.

The first of these was the following night, and she was keyed up for it, aware of the difference. She drove over to pick Mum up straight after dinner, and had her settled in front of television with her oxygen, and Duncan settled in bed with his night-light, by eight. She then dutifully went to bed herself, with the alarm set for twenty past ten. Tonight, she probably wouldn't get any sleep this early, but tomorrow would be a different story.

Sure enough, she spent most of the two hours just lying there, watching the numbers change on the digital clock and thinking circular thoughts about Dylan Calford. She got out of bed before the alarm went off.

The hospital felt different at night, and the theatre

suite even more so. Surgery was limited to emergencies, including Caesarean deliveries, and she arrived in time to hear a newborn crying in its clear plastic cot on its way up in the lift to the maternity ward, one level above.

Occasionally, she might be rostered in Theatre Four for obstetrics, but mostly she'd be across the corridor in Theatre Two or Three, assisting with complicated fractures and closed head injuries, coronary artery bypass grafts and emergency appendicectomies, and putting people back together after accidents. Sometimes she'd see Dylan.

Not tonight, she hoped.

Tonight, she wanted a nice easy start, with some quiet periods in which to grab some sleep.

Occasionally, it seemed, wishes of this selfish kind did come true. They handled emergency surgery on a fifty-seven-year-old man's bowel obstruction, and sewed up a shallow knife wound in another man's chest. The alleged assailant was in police custody. After this, she slept from three until six, then assisted in another stitching up—glass in a woman's foot this time.

The patient had delayed coming in for some hours, the glass was dirty and she wasn't up to date on her tetanus, so it might not be as simple a recovery as it could have been. At least the surgery itself went smoothly.

'Always makes me think of that prissy little proverb about a stitch in time,' commented fellow nurse, Sue Thorpe, stifling a yawn.

Annabelle pulled off her gloves and threw them in the bin, then helped Sue push the patient, on her wheeled bed, out to Recovery. She yawned as well. 'You don't think it's true?' she asked Sue.

'Oh, I'm sure it's true! But it's not always helpful. Sometimes you don't get the chance to put in that first stitch. The whole seam is ripped before you notice a problem.'

'Are we talking about needlework here?'

'Life, darling,' Sue drawled.

Perhaps I needed to hear that, Annabelle thought as they tidied up.

She had been wondering what she could have done to stop herself from feeling the way she did about Dylan—full of regret, still wanting him, still angry with him, wondering what her own problem was and if she was just being irrational—but perhaps there was nothing to learn from going over it all. Somehow, it was inevitable that she should have ended up in a mess. Sometimes, as Sue had said, you didn't notice anything was wrong until the whole seam was ripped.

She heard Dylan's voice just then, penetrating through the theatre's swing doors as they opened again. The anaesthetist, Andrew Brockway, had started to leave, but had turned in the doorway. He held the door open with his shoulder as he mumbled a question to Sue. Beyond him, Dylan's words were clearer.

'What's happening?' He sounded alert, and full of authority. 'Is he ready for us?'

Apparently, he was about to operate in this theatre as soon as the place was cleaned and prepared by the incoming staff.

'Not yet,' said a woman's voice. 'He's still in A and E, getting stabilised. And we've got day shift nursing staff coming on.'

'Who else is operating?'

'Kevin Neeley, since the guy has facial injuries,' said someone else. 'Cam Brewer, too, I think.'

Dylan whistled, then said, 'OK, I'll go and—'

The swing doors closed again as Andrew Brockway left, and Annabelle couldn't hear any more. She assumed they had an accident victim with multiple injuries. Dylan and the rest of his surgical team could be here for hours. She finished up some ten minutes later, and didn't see him on her way out.

That night, after a satisfying snooze on the couch while Duncan watched a video, and a two-hour nap in bed between eight and ten, it was a different story. They had a patient flown in by helicopter, having suffered a serious fall while rock-climbing. His injuries were severe and extensive, and it was obvious at once that it would take all night to patch him up. Dylan would be heavily involved, as the twenty-four-year-old had sustained two complicated spiral fractures of each femur—fractures where the broken bone was protruding through the skin, creating a serious risk of infection—and three more simple breaks.

Meanwhile, a gastric lavage had shown a bleeding spleen. The patient's blood pressure was still dropping slowly, despite the replacement blood going into him, and gastro-intestinal surgeon Cam Brewer had been called in to do a life-saving repair before the less critical orthopaedic procedures could take place.

Dylan, already on hand, looked tired in contrast to the way he'd sounded this morning, Annabelle noted, and she wondered how many hours he'd already spent in surgery today. The large team grouped themselves around the patient, and he seemed unusually terse as he outlined what he needed to do and when he needed to do it.

It was out of character, and Annabelle saw that she wasn't the only one to notice it. Sue Thorpe was working again tonight. She'd had years of experience in the operating theatres at Coronation Hospital, and knew everyone. Divorced and with a couple of grown children, she acted like a cross between an interfering mother and everyone's favourite school teacher.

She also found plenty of time to take in exactly what was going on, and Annabelle caught the sharp, assessing glance she shot at Dylan from across the room as he said shortly, 'No, Cam, I've said that shouldn't be a problem, haven't I? His legs are all right for the moment, and they can wait till you're done. I'll stay on hand until then, just in case we get a further complication. Let's get started, shall we? If you don't repair that tear in the spleen, it'll be academic because he'll have lost too much blood.'

They were already transfusing it in as fast as they could.

The atmosphere didn't get better. Annabelle could see that Dylan was trying to stay calm and pleasant—battling to do so, actually. Even when he spoke cheerfully, it didn't sound natural. Why was it such a struggle? Purely because he was tired? That shouldn't be a problem. He wouldn't have reached this stage in his career if he couldn't function under pressure and fatigue.

Finally, it clicked.

He's in pain.

She was more and more sure of it as the long and gruelling operation proceeded. The patient's condition wasn't good. His blood pressure was dangerously low, and Cam Brewer had to work with total concentration to repair the extensively damaged spleen. Only once that was stitched up and the abdomen closed did the patient's condition improve a little.

'This leg is just lovely!' Dylan muttered, when he was able to get to work at last. He listed a long string of equipment he'd need. Plates and pins of different types. 'I'm doing a damned jigsaw puzzle!'

He *was* in pain.

Annabelle remembered the night he'd looked in her bathroom cabinet for painkillers, and his not-quite-convincing agreement when she'd asked if he had a headache.

They had now reached the most difficult part of Dylan's work—the smashed and twisted left leg, through which a jagged and splintered bone still protruded.

He stepped back. 'I want to call Alex Sturgess for this,' he announced.

'Yeah?' said the resident, David Yan.

Cam Brewer looked surprised, too. They had enough doctors here, including a second orthopaedic registrar, Brian Collins, who wanted the experience. This wasn't one of Alex's private patients and, although it was difficult, it wasn't the kind of surgery that he would expect to be summoned for.

Whatever Dylan was suffering, it must be bad— bad enough to put doubt in his mind as to whether he could safely get through the operation.

Sue had already moved to the wall-mounted phone. 'Could we have Dr Sturgess paged at home, please?' she said.

'I'll keep going,' Dylan said. 'Don't want to wait. He can take over when he gets here.'

'Is there a problem, Dylan?' Cam asked.

Dylan gave a technical answer which made enough sense to satisfy everyone—the complex nature of the pinning and plating required, the fact that both legs were involved, the need for fast work.

Satisfied everyone, that was, except Annabelle.

What was it? Migraine? Vision problems?

Pain. Definitely pain. His mouth looked tight and thin, as if he were tasting vinegar. There were grim lines etched around it, his eyes were suffering, and he was sweating. She could see the dampness at his temples and a shine on his upper lip.

But she couldn't ask him about it. Not now. If he wanted people to know, he would have said something. At least Alex would get here as soon as he could. She knew that from personal experience. He could make it out of his house within two minutes of being called in, even at two or three in the morning, and he always took such calls seriously.

'Yes,' he said when he arrived. 'I'm glad you called me, Calford. This is a good one. Brian, you'll get a lot out of this. Now, the way we're going to do it…'

They were in surgery for another four hours.

The change-room felt blessedly cool. Dylan locked the door and pulled his damp T-shirt over his head. Breath left his body on a shudder of exhaustion. The whole long night had been appalling.

At one point, a couple of hours into the operation, he'd looked ahead to what he still had to do, with a patient who was hovering dangerously close to death, and had thought in panic, I can't! The pain's too bad. I don't feel safe. If I made a mistake…

That was when he had asked for Alex to be called in, and he had to be grateful to the other man for not questioning it. The senior surgeon had worked quickly, and had delegated expertly, showing all of the brilliance that, at times like this, excused his worst behaviour. Now the patient was doing better than they had feared.

'But I'm not,' he muttered. 'I'm not doing very well at all.'

He needed to see someone, get some tests done. The self-diagnosis that had taken him off to the physiotherapist for a bit of massage was obviously off base. He was starting to sketch out the more serious scenarios now. Permanent damage. A malignant growth. A pinched nerve that would never settle back where it belonged.

And if the pain continued, then his career couldn't. He couldn't operate if his back went on feeling like this, day after day. Any medication strong enough to numb the agony would hopelessly compromise his mental acuity and his fine motor control.

Dylan shrugged his shoulders into a business shirt and put on the tie that was hanging in his locker. It was Monday morning, and he had rounds. As soon as they were over, he'd phone a colleague—not Alex, spinal problems weren't his area in any case—and ask to be seen.

Kemp McAllister, as first choice. Simon Grant as back-up. This morning, if possible. A professional favour. Now that he'd made up his mind this was serious, he wanted to know the full story as soon as he could.

Annabelle was hovering outside the change-room. Waiting for him? Looked like it. Instantly, there was the usual current of electricity and perception between them. She looked tired, but her eyes were wide and dark, and he was flooded with the warmth of her concern.

'You're in pain,' she said at once. 'I could tell, all through the operation. Where, Dylan? What is it?'

'It's my back,' he muttered. 'Don't let's talk about it here.'

She must have thought he meant, Let's talk about it somewhere else, because she nodded straight away and said, 'Want to grab a quick coffee? I'm a little bit late, but Mum knows that can happen sometimes. Another twenty minutes won't hurt.'

'All right,' he agreed. He wanted it, suddenly. Wanted *her*, sitting across the table from him and listening while he talked it out.

'Just let me change,' she said, and was in and out within three minutes. She'd exchanged the night's limp theatre suit for a pastel top and skirt, and she looked as cool and fresh as a flower.

They found the quietest corner of the hospital's public café, and she set her caffe latte down on the table in front of her, leaned across it and touched his hand. 'Are you afraid it's something serious?'

'I'm— Yes.' He let out a sigh, but kept the worst of his feelings bottled in. No point in admitting to the full range of panicky scenarios that filled his mind. 'It's too soon to think that way,' he said, more decisively. 'I haven't seen anyone yet. But the pain was…pretty bad last night. I didn't want anyone to guess.'

'No one did. Except me. You hid it pretty well. Sue knew something was bothering you, but she shrugged it off, I think. Put it down to fatigue, and the surgery you'd had earlier in the day. Has it been coming on for a while? Was that why you were delving in my medicine cabinet that night?'

'Yes.'

'You said it was a headache.'

'No, I let you say it, and I didn't contradict you. That's not quite so bad, as lies go!'

There was a silence. Dylan thought about the night some more, and was certain that she was thinking about it, too. The first night they'd slept together. One of far too few such nights, full of a promise and delight that hadn't been fulfilled because she'd finished it. She'd had reasons. He conceded that. But should those reasons have been deal-breakers?

Missed connections like this just…*happened* in today's world. At the moment, it seemed like an enormous waste, and he couldn't help feeling angry about it.

'Look, phone me, won't you?' Annabelle said. Her voice wasn't quite steady. Her coffee was already almost gone. She was gulping it down. 'Tell me the news. Or come over to my place. I really mean that, Dylan. If you need to talk.'

To *talk*?

She was leaning forward, her eyes big and warm and her mouth full with compassion. Another inch, and their fingers would have touched. Another six inches, and he could have captured that mouth in a long, deep kiss. Except…

Talking? That was what she was offering?

'No, thanks,' he answered.

'Oh.' She sat back a little, having sensed his rebuff with ease.

Well, good!

Hell, *talking?*

If she was going to reach out, he wanted a heck of a lot more from her than that! He wanted to take hold of that soft, pretty hand and squeeze it. He wanted to feel her fingers lacing through his and stroking his skin. He wanted each touch to contain the erotic promise of sex, and a lot more besides.

Angry with her, he scalded his throat with the last mouthful of his black espresso and stood up.

'Rounds,' he said. 'With the other business, my back, I'll keep you posted.'

'Dylan...' She stood up as well, and followed him. 'If there's anything you need, don't hesitate to ask, OK?'

And that was when he totally lost it.

'Is that the only role you feel safe with, Annabelle? Is it too frightening to have wants and needs of your own? You practically threw me out the door because I gave you a bit of help. Not meant as a transaction of any kind. Just because I cared. And you couldn't take it. But now that you get the chance to be saintly Sister Drew again, you're right at home. What kind of an avoidance strategy have you got going there?'

'I'm not in the least saintly.' She flushed. 'I— And I certainly don't want to be!'

'I used to think that about you—that the title of Sister fitted you, as if there was still that Florence Nightingale aura around you. And I think I was right.'

'That's an insult, Dylan.'

'Is it? Deal with it! For a while, just recently, I thought I was wrong. Alex dropping you at your own wedding jolted you out of your accustomed role for a while, but now you're getting another chance to hide inside it again. No, there's nothing I "need",

OK? Nothing that you're offering, anyway. On the other hand, there's plenty that I want. I think you know what I mean. Let me know if the situation changes, and I might still be interested.'

She nodded slowly. She looked stricken, and he felt a twist of remorse inside him, but she said nothing, and he wasn't going to wait any longer. As he left the café, he didn't give her a backward glance.

'Nothing showed up on the CAT scan, Dylan,' said Kemp McAllister. 'Your spine is in great condition.' He amplified the statement with technical language, because he rightly guessed that Dylan would want full detail. 'Look at the pictures yourself later on.'

He slid the big envelope containing the images from the scan across his desk, then gave the announcement that Dylan had expected.

'I'm going to send you for an MRI. It's still possible there's a tumour that the CAT scan didn't pick up.'

'Pressing on the nerve.'

'That's right. The sailing trip might have caused some temporary, localised inflammation, which increased the pressure on the nerve and caused that first bout of pain. As the inflammation subsided, the pain did, too. But if there is a tumour and it's growing…'

'The pain is back again, and increasing, even without the earlier inflammation,' Dylan finished.

He didn't need to ask any more questions or hear any more explanations from Kemp. He knew as much as the other man did now. Too many ifs. *If* there was a tumour at all. *If* it was operable. *If* it was operable, but so integrally connected to the spinal cord that its removal would leave him with loss of function in his legs...

And before any of those 'ifs' could be eliminated, there was the MRI.

Although he'd never had one himself, he knew exactly what was involved—total immobility for well over half an hour in an extremely confined and painfully noisy cylinder of high-tech machinery, while his back was scanned in minute cross-sections and an image was generated.

The procedure wasn't painful—if you didn't count the assault on the eardrums—but many people found the sense of confinement, immobility and powerlessness quite terrifying. He'd had one patient recently who had shaken so much that the scan had been almost useless.

Dylan wasn't a big fan of confined spaces. For preference, he would have chosen pain.

He cleared his throat. 'When can they fit me in? Any idea?'

'I'll call the imaging centre myself and try to get a cancellation for you. First available chance, Dylan, don't worry.'

'What do you really think, Kemp?'

'Truth? I've seen tumours presenting like this. I've even seen septicaemia presenting like this—abscesses pressing on the spine.'

'I very much doubt it's septicaemia!'

'I agree. That was just an illustration. But let's wait for the MRI before we conjecture any further.'

The wait took four days. Finally, on Friday at seven-thirty in the morning, he got a hurried call from Kemp saying, 'Short notice—I meant to call you last night—but if you can clear your schedule for this afternoon, the imaging centre can fit you in at three.'

'Three today?' Get Brian to cover the last two hours of his fracture clinic. Should be fine. 'Thanks, Kemp.'

Putting down the phone, he turned to find Annabelle emerging from the nurses' change-room in her street clothes after her eleven till seven shift in Theatre Two.

'I'm sorry,' she said. 'I couldn't help— Was that Kemp McAllister you were talking to?' He didn't reply at once, and she went on hurriedly, 'I wasn't eavesdropping. I just heard you say his name. And I was hoping you'd phone, Dylan. I've been…thinking about it…about you…all week.'

'I've got an MRI booked for three o'clock this afternoon,' he told her.

There was no point in prolonging the conversation by trying to duck her interest. They'd slept together. They'd had the beginnings of a relationship. There was still a pull. A *huge* pull, if he was honest, despite the fact that any anger between them definitely went both ways, now. He'd been fairly brutal to her on Monday, and he wasn't sorry about it.

'OK,' was all she said. Those usual big, warm eyes. That usual slow, careful nod. Then she added, 'I'll be thinking of you, Dylan.'

'If you think it'll help,' he drawled, laying the sarcasm on thickly.

'Yes, I think it will,' she retorted, colour warming her cheeks like two ripe peaches.

'Good for you,' he muttered. He turned away down the corridor without waiting to see if she'd heard.

Surprising how much it hurt to be angry with her,

like sandpaper rubbing on sunburned skin. The long morning of surgery he headed into five minutes later came as a relief.

Duncan loved his first morning at playgroup. It was held at a local church hall with plenty of toys, a shady fenced yard, a sand-pit and climbing equipment. He was wary at first, and clung to Annabelle tightly.

She didn't quite know why he was doing it, but relished his need and their closeness. Dylan had hurt her this morning. Angered her, too, the way he'd angered and hurt her on Monday morning with his accusations about saintliness and hiding. Could there be any truth in what he'd said? She had been thinking about it all week, but didn't have any clear answers.

Something to do with her feelings about Vic. She'd known for a while that some of her actions and her decisions were direct responses to how she felt about Vic's way of approaching life.

Vic had lurched from one career path to another—journalism, modelling, web-site design, catering. Although it hadn't seemed to bother her, she'd never stuck at anything long enough to get good at it, or to make any money.

Annabelle herself, in contrast, had enrolled in nursing and had never deflected from her original goals.

Vic had fallen passionately, ecstatically and painfully in love several times a year. On cloud nine while the affair was at maximum sizzle, pit of despair when it ended...until the next exotic and unlikely lover came along. As well as the Greek barman, there had been a surf-shop owner, a garage mechanic, a singer in a band, a TV news cameraman—more men than Annabelle could tally up.

Annabelle, on the other hand, had had a couple of cautious relationships with cautious men, both of which had ended by mutual agreement before anyone had become too deeply involved. Alex's departure from their wedding had been the only romantic event that could have vied for dramatic content with Vic's flamboyant history of affairs.

Vic had been her own woman, answerable to no one, in charge of her decisions and in charge of her life. Independent. Self-sufficient.

Annabelle had always looked to other people— their needs, their approval.

Except…

That was only Vic's perception, she realised as Duncan showed her the star shapes he was making with pink play dough. How independent was Vic really? With everything she did, someone else had to pick up the pieces for her afterwards.

Annabelle had made calls to Vic's catering clients to cancel their bookings and recommend another firm. 'I'm sorry, Belle. I'm rotten at this. I'm losing money hand over fist. And I can't face those people.' She'd cleaned Vic's flat when Vic had broken her lease to go overseas. 'I just don't have time. The best flight deal I could get has me flying out Monday. Getting away is going to give me some perspective, and I really need that right now!'

And Annabelle had inherited Duncan.

Vic hadn't been independent and self-reliant. She'd been lost. She hadn't had a clue what she'd wanted, or what she'd been doing, and if other people hadn't been there to help, her life had fallen apart.

'Mummy staying?' Duncan asked her, still snuggled, uncharacteristically, on her lap as they sat at the play-dough table.

She realised that he thought playgroup was like child-care, and he was expecting—and dreading—her departure. She felt a rush of love, and hugged him tightly. 'Yes, I'm staying,' she told him. 'I'm always going to stay with you at playgroup.'

'Mummy always stay at playgroup,' he said happily. He dropped the play dough at once and ran off outside to explore.

His departure left her free to wonder what any of that stuff about Vic had to do with Dylan's accusations, until she got caught up in conversation with the other parents and carers while they had coffee. One of the mothers looked familiar, and after a bit of speculating and memory-jogging, they finally realised that Gina was the younger sister of one of Annabelle's old school-mates.

'Laurie will want to know all about what you're doing now,' she said, and Annabelle ended up telling everyone much more than she'd expected to about Duncan's difficult start and her own current determination to put his needs first in her life.

'You're crazy, trying to make that schedule work!' one of the women said. 'You'll kill yourself!'

But everyone else was supportive. They talked about sleep disruption with a new baby, and their own decisions about child-care and conflicts regarding working versus staying at home. It felt good. Duncan came up to her frequently—for a hug when he hurt himself, for a push on the swing, for dispute resolution when he and another boy both wanted to ride the same tricycle.

Gina said to Annabelle quietly a little later, 'I don't

agree with Ella that you're going to kill yourself, but you do look tired. Joshie and Duncan seem to be playing nicely together. If you ever want to drop him over for a few hours while you grab a sleep or get some errands done, feel free. We all tend to help each other out that way. This afternoon, if you want to.'

This afternoon, when Dylan had his MRI.

Annabelle hesitated at first. Dylan had been pretty rude, and pretty dampening, about her assumption that she had something of value to give. Why should she show up to hold his hand?

Because no one else would.

He had no family here, and she was sure he'd told as few people as possible about his back pain. He certainly wasn't the kind of man who'd trouble a male friend for support. The mates he'd gone sailing with a few weeks ago would probably be the last people to hear about the problem with his back.

Perhaps we both find it harder to take support than to give it, she thought.

On the face of it, an MRI was a simple, non-invasive test, but she knew one nurse who'd sworn she'd rather 'get eaten by a crocodile' than go through one again.

'Actually, Gina…' Annabelle said, and they fixed it up in a couple of minutes.

She would drop Duncan at Gina's at three-ish, and pick him up again on the way to Mum's at around five. Time for some shopping, some cleaning, a short nap…or a stop at the imaging clinic to see Dylan.

'How did you go?' the receptionist asked.

'It was fine,' the young woman said cheerfully. 'It's a cool machine.'

She leaned on the desk, looking in her backpack for her purse. She wore a black top and skin tight black trousers that rode low on her hips, she had hair the shade of blue food colouring and a very high metal content on various tender parts of her anatomy. On her, the look worked. So did the cheerfulness and the insouciance.

Dylan would have purchased some of it from her, if that were possible. He wondered why she had needed the scan. Something gynaecological? If she was concerned about the result, she wasn't letting it show.

'Dr Calford?' said the technician, appearing in the doorway which led away from the waiting room.

It is ridiculous to feel so nervous!

At the moment, it was the scan itself, but underlying this and strongly colouring Dylan's emotional state was his knowledge that the result could shatter his life. He felt very alone in the face of that knowledge.

It's going to be fine. Cool. Just like the young woman with blue hair had said.

It wasn't.

He hated everything about it. Hated wearing the hospital gown. Hated the antiseptic white of the MRI scanner, inside and out. He hated going in head first, and he hated its tight fit. Heaven only knew how a man with shoulders any broader than his would have squeezed through. He hated the mesh-like cage at his face. He hated the constant white light, and the fact that he wasn't supposed to move a muscle.

Most of all, he hated the noise. Yes, it really was like athletic shoes going round and round in a tumble dryer—a dryer that was tumbling around Dylan himself. As his body was fed slowly, sl-o-owly through the long tube and he ached with the effort of lying still, it felt like time itself had slowed to a standstill.

When he finally emerged, he knew he must be as white as the machine. He felt ill, drained of adrenalin, deafened and off-balance. Getting dressed was such an effort that the technician knocked on the door after a few minutes to see if he was still breathing. She found him sitting there with his shoes in his hand and his head between his knees.

'Are you all right, Dr Calford?'

'Getting there.'

'Yes, it does bother some people.'

Some people, it didn't. The next patient, a frail-looking man of about sixty-five, who seemed completely at ease in his lemon yellow floral hospital gown, poked his head around the door and chuckled at Dylan.

'Doesn't worry me a bit,' he claimed. 'I had one a couple of years ago. Planning to fall asleep in there this time.'

Dylan raised his head and the room tilted and blurred. 'Good for you,' he said.

The man shuffled off, still chuckling.

'Do you have someone waiting for you?' the technician asked.

'No.'

'And you're driving yourself?'

'Yes. I'll be fine.'

'Better wait a while,' she said. 'Have a cuppa. One of the reception staff will be very happy to make one for you.'

'Might do that,' he agreed. He felt dizzy, as if he

himself had been one of the athletic shoes tumbling in the dryer.

Determined not to give in to it, he put his shoes on and walked out to the waiting room. He knew he probably looked like a drunken man—one who was convinced against all evidence that he was walking a straight line. He didn't care.

And then he saw Annabelle.

CHAPTER NINE

DYLAN was scowling at her, Annabelle noted at once.

Or was he just fighting to see straight?

She almost scowled back, not sure now why she had come. She was sure he wouldn't welcome her, even if he fell into the group of people who found MRIs to be difficult. His face told her she was right on both counts. It had been difficult, and he didn't want her. His expression had set hard, and he wasn't smiling.

'Hi,' he said, speaking through a narrow slit in his lips.

'Hi.' She was almost as prickly as he was. 'Looks like I should get you a cup of tea or something. I can drive you home, too, if you like.'

'I'll be fine in a minute. The tech said I could ask at the desk for some tea.'

'I'll ask. Or there's a café next level down if you want brewed coffee and don't mind a styrofoam cup.'

'Whatever. Tea, but I don't care where it comes from.'

She hesitated, then decided to ask at the desk. Styrofoam cups were horrible. She touched Dylan's shoulder, then looked for a sign from him that it was OK to do more. Hug him. Sit down beside him and stroke his thigh for a moment, or lay her head against his chest. But he didn't give her any such sign. Just sat there, doing a very good impression of a man who was feeling perfectly all right.

'When do you get the—?' she began.

He cut in without letting her finish. 'Oberlin—Paul Oberlin, the radiologist—is going to courier the pictures over to Kemp McAllister as soon as he's done his report. If I know Kemp, he'll completely ignore the report anyway, and analyse the images himself. He should phone me by the end of the day.'

'I'll get you that tea.'

He didn't thank her until she put the hot mug in his hand, and even then it was only a grunted word. 'You didn't need to come,' he added.

'I wanted to. But I can't stay long. One of the playgroup mums has Duncan, and I'm not sure how it's going to work out. It's the first time he's played there. May I...uh...phone you tomorrow morning, to hear what Paul Oberlin and Kemp McAllister have said?'

He looked at her properly at last, and growled, 'Of course you can, Annabelle. It's not going to stay a secret for much longer, in any case, whatever it is.'

'OK, then.'

She sat down beside him, but didn't touch him the way she wanted to. The space between their bodies felt thick and uncomfortable, and they didn't even talk until he asked, 'How's Duncan?'

'Oh, we've had a great time together this week.'

'You look tired.'

'So I've been told! I'm expecting to look tired for a while. New parents manage it. Plenty of people manage it.'

'Don't let it get to breaking point. You're only human.'

'I know that, Dylan.'

They looked at each other helplessly for a second

or two, then both turned away, unable to bridge the gap. She left a few minutes later.

'Listen, Dylan,' Kemp said on the phone, 'I know you'll want to see these for yourself—'

'Yes, but I also want the bottom line right now, if you can give it to me.'

His stomach was flipping like a fish on dry land, and he hoped it wasn't obvious in his voice. The phone call had come later than he'd expected. The specialist had got caught up in other matters. It was after eight in the evening, and Dylan had spent the past two hours sweating and watching the clock.

'OK, yes, I thought that's what you'd say. Bottom line is that, yes, something showed up. A tumour. From the evidence on the scan, it's not obviously malignant, just a benign nerve tumour a little over a centimetre in diameter, but, of course, we won't know for certain until we've taken it out and had a good look at it. Now, the bad news is—'

Dylan swore. 'That was the *good* news?'

'Well, yes. The thing that concerns me is its position, so close to the nerves. You've got to get it removed, but you may end up with nerve deficits in your legs as a result.'

Nerve deficits in his legs. A polite, technical way of saying that he wouldn't be able to walk properly, or stand for long periods. He wouldn't be able to do his job. You couldn't perform surgery if you couldn't stand.

'If we get Graham Barlow to operate…' Dylan suggested, starting to sweat.

'Yes, that's who I'd recommend. From the way your symptoms have developed, it's growing relatively fast, so we should move forward on the surgery as soon as possible. I've already spoken to Graham, and he can fit you in next Friday. Does that give you enough time to clear your schedule?'

'It'll have to. I don't want to wait on this.'

'Obviously, it's awful for you.'

'I'll get through it. Thanks, Kemp.'

'Get in touch if you have questions. Anything you want to talk about.'

'Thanks,' Dylan said again.

He didn't phone anyone after he'd finished talking to Kemp. Not his parents, or his sister, or his friends. Distantly, he realised that it might be a good idea, but somehow he couldn't do it. Didn't want to have to tell the whole story, or hear the emotional, appalled responses he'd get when he outlined the two worst-case scenarios—malignancy and damaged nerves.

The only person he really wanted to phone was Annabelle. Not to tell her, but to ask her whether he could come round.

Can I bury myself in your body and anaesthetise myself in your arms? Can I take nourishment from the smell of your hair and the sound of your voice? Can I sit beside you in utter silence and feel your care?

He even thought it very likely that she wouldn't turn him away from her bed tonight. She would sense his need, and that would be enough.

Enough for her. Not enough for him.

Annabelle hoped Dylan would phone that night, but he didn't. She went to work at eleven, leaving Mum already asleep in her tiny third bedroom, but she knew Dylan wasn't on call tonight.

Things were fairly quiet until around three in the morning, when they had to call in a cardiothoracic surgeon to perform an emergency coronary artery by-pass, and she got away promptly at seven.

Dylan had told her yesterday that 'of course' she could phone him that morning, but she didn't want to disturb him early. If he'd had a bad night... In the end, she waited until eleven and by then he'd gone out. She didn't leave a message on his machine.

Several more tries over the course of the day got the same result, and she began to wonder if he was screening his calls. It was eight in the evening before she finally reached him, when Duncan was already in bed and Mum was watching her evening television shows.

He knew what she wanted to ask him, and launched into his account straight away. His wooden tone only served to outline his words in darker colours, and she couldn't hold back a stricken cry when he told her the worst possibilities.

'Have you talked to your parents about this?' she asked.

'Not yet.'

'Your sister? Your friends?'

'No. I'll tell Alex, of course. He'll need to know. I've been trying to get hold of him, but he hasn't returned my calls yet.'

'Have you told Sarah?'

He laughed at this. 'No!'

'At some point—'

'I'll tell people after the surgery. When I know. Why tie anyone else in knots with worry when there's nothing they can do? Why have everyone at the hospital buzzing with speculation? My parents would probably fly out—'

'Of course! You should give them that option,' she urged him. 'Don't make their decisions for them.'

He sighed. 'Listen, it's my decision, not theirs. I want to see them. When I know how well I can walk, and whether I'm going to live.' Oh, dear God! 'That's when I want to see them. Until then—'

'You've only got me,' she said softly, her voice catching in her throat.

'Yeah, and you'd get out of my face if you had any sense!'

'Well, maybe I haven't any sense where you're concerned.'

Dylan made a disgusted sound. 'Leave it, Annabelle. I mean that. Leave me alone. Ask yourself why you're only interested now that I'm facing this, now that I'm needy and not so strong.'

'You're still strong, Dylan!'

He ignored her. 'Is it safer for you that way? Does it fit with the way you see yourself? Because it doesn't fit with what *I* want! As you said to me a few weeks ago in a different context, I'm not your charity.'

'No,' she agreed, her voice tight. 'You're not. That's not what this is about.'

He laughed again—the same cynical, dismissive sound she'd heard just now when she'd asked if he'd told Sarah. This link with his ex-wife was, Annabelle knew, anything but flattering. When she put down the phone a minute later, she felt totally shut out of his life.

And she knew fully, for the first time, that she was in love with him.

That was the difference. That was the key. This wasn't about her instinct—too well developed, at times; perhaps he was right about that—to respond to the needs of others and deny what she needed for herself. This was pure selfishness. She loved him, and she wanted to be with him, share this with him, whatever the outcome was. Except that he seemed to be telling her that it was too late.

'How are your shifts now? Busy?' Barb Thompson asked Annabelle.

The two of them had overlapped briefly in the theatre suite. It was Monday morning, and Annabelle was finishing work while Barb was just starting.

'Usually pretty busy,' she answered. 'Sometimes we get a good break. But the pace is hectic, since they're all emergency procedures.'

'Enjoying it, though?'

'Yes, actually. More than I'd expected to. I was really only focusing on the hours. The drama can be satisfying, and when we get a good outcome against the odds it really feels good.'

Good enough to carry her through several tiring days with Duncan, slotted in between her shifts. But only just good enough. She yawned. Now she had three nights in a row in which to get some deep, solid sleep—if she wasn't thinking too much about Dylan.

His own surgery was this coming Friday, but he hadn't wanted her support.

'I just looked at today's list,' Barb said. 'We've got Jason Gregory's knee reconstruction first up.'

'Is Dylan operating?' Annabelle had to ask.

'No, and I was a little surprised about that,' Barb answered. 'Apparently, he's off for the next two weeks. No one seems to know why. Sturgess…that is, Alex…is doing it. In fact, he's already here, somewhere about.'

'It's a difficult operation,' Annabelle said, as neutrally as she could. She knew, of course, why Alex was doing it, but if Dylan didn't want anyone to know what was going on until after his own surgery, she had to respect that.

Barb went back to making her preparations for the morning's list, and Annabelle began to remove her disposable shoe covers, then paused. She could hear Alex's voice, talking to someone on the phone as he waited until the patient was brought down and it was time to scrub.

She didn't need to talk to Alex about the surgery. Jason Gregory was just another patient.

Yes, but he was Dylan's patient, and his professional future mirrored Dylan's own fears about what lay in store for him.

Fighting down her reluctance, she walked across the wide corridor of the theatre suite, to where Alex stood talking on a wall-mounted phone. He replaced the receiver in its cradle just as she neared him, and he would have walked off if she hadn't spoken his name.

'Alex…'

It was the first time she'd used his first name since the day after their cancelled wedding, when she'd phoned him and begged him for a chance to talk.

'Yes?' He turned back to her warily.

'I just heard that you were doing Jason Gregory's surgery this morning.'

'That's right.'

'Are you handling all Dylan's lists over the next two weeks?'

'A couple of them. Brian Collins is doing some. And Keith Shartles's registrar, Lucas North.'

'I know about Dylan's tumour.'

There was a tiny silence. 'Then you're one of the few who does,' Alex said.

'Yes. I—I know that, too.'

'Make sure you keep it that way.'

'I just wanted to say I hope it goes well with Jason Gregory's knee, that's all.'

'He's realistic about what to expect. He's got plans to buy into a tourist development at Port Douglas, apparently.'

'Dylan was concerned about how he'd adjust.'

'Better than Dylan will himself, I expect, if he has the same outcome. A surgeon plans for a longer career than a rugby player.' Alex shifted his shoulders and his weight, as if he was about to walk away, but then he stopped and said quietly, 'About what happened in January... Would you have preferred a divorce further down the track, Annabelle? Because that's what it would have come to. I could suddenly see it, right in that moment after Dylan spoke. I could see it wasn't going to work for us. It was...histrionic of me to blame you and Calford. Then, and later.'

Should I tell him about our affair? Annabelle wondered.

Why, though? It had begun well after Alex had departed from her private life, and it was already over.

'I should apologise for that,' Alex went on. 'I *am* apologising for it,' he amended impatiently. 'The scrub who's replaced you isn't nearly as good. Never anticipates what I want.'

'That's not why I changed shifts, Alex. It wasn't because of us. Or not directly.'

'Yes, well…' He looked at his watch. 'No hard feelings now. Things are OK.'

'Yes.'

'For us, if not for poor Calford.'

She couldn't help protesting, 'There's a chance the tumour can be removed with no damage to the nerves.'

'Yes, but they're not odds I'd take on a horse at the racetrack! No wonder he's taken this week off! I wouldn't like to operate while wondering if it was the last time I'd ever be able to do it.'

'I think he was afraid the pain would compromise his performance.'

'That, too,' Alex agreed.

They both saw the plastic doors open at the end of the corridor at that moment. Jason Gregory had been wheeled down from the ward and was ready for his surgery.

Annabelle spent a good day with Duncan—if a little more active than she really had the energy for—and dropped in for an hour at Mum's. Four days from now, Dylan's surgery would be over.

That night, she was so tired that she slept long and well, from nine in the evening until Duncan's little feet running down the passage woke her the following morning at six. They did laundry, ran errands and swam in the morning, and in the afternoon she had Gina and Joshie over to play.

She and Gina had cool drinks together, talking eas-ily the whole time. At school, so long ago, their age difference of two years had seemed considerable, but now it didn't matter at all. Laurie, who had then been Annabelle's friend, was living on a cattle station in the centre of the state, and she had children, too.

'Which most of my friends don't,' Annabelle said. 'And no one I know who lives close. There are a few kids in this street, but they're school-age.'

'Compatible kids. That's what friendships are based on when you're a parent,' Gina said with a laugh.

'Speaking of which, would you like to leave Joshie here for the rest of the afternoon, and have some time to yourself? I'll feel more comfortable about leaving Duncan with you sometimes if I get to reciprocate.'

'Well, since I did a pregnancy test last week, and it was positive…'

'Oh, congratulations! That's wonderful!'

'It is…and I'm already starting to feel as if I got run over by a bus, so I'll very happily take you up on your offer!' Gina finished.

The two little boys played together with no conflict, after she'd gone, for nearly three hours.

Three days until Dylan's surgery.

On Wednesday, Linda—old friend, financial adviser and thwarted bridesmaid—dropped in for a quick lunch between business meetings.

'Can I do this sometimes?' she asked. She pulled off the tailored jacket of her conservative navy suit and hung it on the back of the kitchen door. 'It's so nice to know you'll often be home during the day!'

She made awkward small talk for a while as they sat on the edge of Duncan's sand-pit, watching him play while they ate ham and salad sandwiches, then suddenly the real reason for her visit came flooding out in a rush.

'I'm seeing someone. It's serious. He wants to marry me. But he wants kids, and I don't know what to say. You know, Rob never wanted them…'

Rob was Linda's previous boyfriend, and he'd never been quite good enough for her, in Annabelle's private opinion.

'And so I kind of got used to thinking I didn't want them either. I don't know *anything* about kids!'

'Nobody does, until they have one,' Annabelle answered. 'Because "kids" in the abstract don't count. It's only *your* kid, and in that area, no matter how the kid is acquired, we all start from square one. So don't let that worry you.'

'But—but—'

'Do you love him, Linda?'

'Uh, yeah, I do,' Linda muttered. 'It's ridiculous, really!'

She was blushing.

'Then make a leap of faith. Marry him, and try for a baby. Life's full of twists and turns.'

'You think so?' The sun came out on Linda's face. 'You think it's that simple?'

Did she? Annabelle wondered. Her turn to talk now. About some of the things she'd been thinking lately about Vic. Vic had believed so completely that she should follow her heart…only her heart had led her on such a wild, erratic dance. Witnessing this, Annabelle had never dared to do the same. But she was starting to see things differently now. Vic hadn't been completely wrong in the way she'd lived her short, flamboyant life.

'Following my heart doesn't have to mean changing lovers and careers and life goals every few months, the way Vic did,' she told Linda. 'It doesn't have to mean messing things up so that other people are left to pick up the pieces. My heart gives steadier signals, I think. Vic did have a lot of courage, in her way. You have to take the leap, and assume you'll have what it takes to follow through when the time comes.'

They couldn't talk about it any more just then. Linda had to put her suit jacket back on and get to her meeting. But their conversation left Annabelle with plenty to think about.

And Dylan was having his surgery in two days.

'Mum, Duncan's in bed and half asleep, already,' Annabelle announced to her mother on Thursday evening at ten past eight.

'Little darling! I'll creep in and kiss him once he's safely off.'

'Would you mind if I head out now? I want to drop in on a friend before I go to work.' Her heart flipped as she said it. Would Dylan consider himself a friend?

'Of course, love. It's nice for you to get out. Is it Linda?'

'No, someone from the hospital.'

She didn't even want to say his name. Wasn't sure why she was doing this. She hadn't seen him all week, and he hadn't phoned. They'd ended their last conversation in anger and distance. Several times, she'd thought of phoning him. Twice she'd keyed in the first few digits of his number, but then she'd stopped. After her talk with Linda today, though…

It was time she took the leap of faith that she'd urged on her old friend.

I was wrong to make such an issue about the bills he paid, and about that leering garage mechanic with his 'doctor boyfriend' line. Dylan caught me on the raw, and I couldn't see it then. Maybe it's too late, but I'll never know if I don't try...

She was dressed casually in jeans and a cotton knit top, ready to change into theatre gear once she got to the hospital at just before eleven. It was tempting to dress up a little, but she resisted it. What would she be trying to prove? And anyway, she didn't have un-limited time. He must be very tense tonight. If he did want to talk it all out...

But when she rang his doorbell, she thought at first that he wasn't even home. After ringing it a second time and waiting in vain, she'd actually turned to leave before she heard the sound of a lock clicking open behind her. He had been in the pool. He wore baggy black swim shorts, water glistened on his skin and there was a towel draped around his neck.

For a moment, neither of them spoke.

'Come in,' he growled at her finally, and stepped back to hold the door open.

'OK,' she bleated, and spent the whole walk through his elegant, masculine townhouse thinking, 'Why am I here? He doesn't want me.'

When they reached the living room, which flowed seamlessly out to a beautifully landscaped courtyard and pool, he offered her something to drink. She chose coffee, thinking of the long night ahead, then added, 'How was your swim?'

'Nice. It's a mild night.'

'Finish your laps. Don't let me interrupt.'

'Time I got out.'

'Get dressed, then. I'll make the coffee.'

Dylan showed her roughly where everything was— this was the first time she'd been to his home—and disappeared into his bedroom, and she was left with the same regret as before. Leaps of faith were all very well in the abstract, but there was no guarantee that you wouldn't make a hard landing.

By the time he returned, Annabelle had the electric kettle boiled and the coffee brewing. He wore jeans and a T-shirt, and hadn't bothered with shoes.

'I suppose you've come to hold my hand,' he said.

Was it a challenge, or just an attack? Either way, it made Annabelle bristle as she poured the coffee into two mugs.

'No, I haven't,' she said.

'So you're not thinking about the fact that I have surgery tomorrow?'

'Of course I am!'

'Then why *are* you here? From the time we've spent together, I'd say there are limited options, and you've just denied the only one that's obvious. I overheard Alex calling me "poor Calford" today.'

It sounded like a *non sequitur*, but Annabelle followed his transition easily—he didn't want anyone's pity. Not Alex's, and not hers.

'You were at the hospital?' she asked inadequately.

'I dropped in to see Jason. He's doing well.' He took the mug she slid across to him, but didn't lift it to his lips. Her own steaming brew was still sitting on the bench-top in front of her as well.

'That's a good omen, I guess,' she said.

He laughed, and it was a harsh, angry sound. 'Do you really think I believe in omens like that?' He swore—a couple of short, pithy words. 'Why are you here, Annabelle? To mouth platitudes? Hell, I hope not! Leave now, if that's the case, because I don't think I could take it tonight.'

'All right.' She took a deep breath. 'You want to know why I'm here?'

Her heart was hammering, and she was angry at how prickly he was, how hard he was making this for her, but she didn't let it sway her. Instead, she deliberately skirted around the protective barrier of the kitchen's black granite bench-top and went up to him. She closed her fingers around his upper arm. The gesture was a demand, but also a caress. His angry prowling ceased.

'*This* is why I'm here,' she said. 'I want you, Dylan. I don't have platitudes, or a hand for you to hold. I just want to be here with you, in the hour and a half before I have to go to work, and if you don't want that, I'll leave.'

His eyes narrowed. 'This is sudden.'

'No! It's not sudden. You know that none of what we felt…none of the desire and the connection…went away when I yelled at you about the garage mechanic and my mother's bills. I overreacted that day. We could have got past it if I'd left the door open. I'm sorry I didn't do that, and I'm here to try again. I'm not thinking of the future. I—I just…want you.'

Love you. Too scary to say it, in case he didn't say it back. She felt it. It burned inside her. But she contented herself with saying the other part.

'I want you, Dylan,' she repeated, on a whisper this time.

He had frozen beneath that one touch of her fingers on his arm, and for a long moment she thought he was going to shake her off and turn away.

'Do you offer this service to all pre-operative patients?' he asked finally. Too silkily.

'No!'

'Then I'm special.'

'Yes. You are. If you don't know that, you're wilfully blind. Do you enjoy making this so hard for me?'

Surely he could *hear* her heart beating by now! How long before he would answer?

Never. He never answered. Or not with words. Instead, a hand dropped to her hip, anchoring her in place as he took one small step, closing the space between them. She looked up into his face and saw the way his dark eyes glittered. Was he still angry?

Surely not. Not when he was about to kiss her. She could see it on his mouth, feel it in the tiny puff of breath that warmed her lower lip. They were only a fraction of an inch apart now. She closed her eyes before his lips touched hers, too churned up with emotion to look at him, and when her eyes were closed, she forgot any thought of his anger.

How could he be angry, when he kissed her like this?

He tasted mint fresh, and his body still felt cool and hard from his swim. His arms wrapped around her, as solid as steel bands. They kissed for a long time, and it felt like magic—like an oasis at the end of a desert journey, like hot food on a wet night, like coming home.

His hands loosened around her body and began to drift, stroking the sensitive skin where her waist curved in, rising higher to brush beneath her breasts then capture them greedily in his hands. He unclipped her bra and they both groaned at the same time as he filled his cupped palms with her weight.

He lifted her top higher and thumbed her hard, exposed nipples, then lowered his head and took her into the warm, wet cavern of his mouth. She shuddered, arched her back and spread her fingers in his hair.

There was no possibility of going slowly now. He gorged hungrily on her breasts and she held onto him like a life-raft in a turbulent current. His capable body seemed like the only fixed point in a swirling, pulsating universe.

'I want to take you to bed,' he muttered. 'This isn't enough, Annabelle.'

'No…'

'*No?*'

'I mean, yes. It isn't enough. Yes, let's go to bed.'

They barely made it. Her top and bra fell onto the living-room floor, and his T-shirt marked the doorway to his room. They stopped there and he pressed her against the wall, his thigh between hers, his mouth on her mouth and his hands everywhere.

She unzipped his jeans and stroked him—warm satin on tempered steel. His ragged response sent her closer to the edge, and she was the one to drag on his naked hips, pulling him to the bed.

Tipping herself backwards, she brought him down on top of her, ready for him, melting and aching for him. He slid inside her and they began to move together, and the coil of tension within her mounted and mounted, threatening to shatter. When she heard him cry out, she thought at first that he'd left her behind, but the sharp sound he made wasn't a sound of pleasure. Frozen in place, he gasped out, 'Stop! Stop!' And she understood.

'It hurts, Dylan?'

'Yes!' He swore. 'Too damn much! I didn't want to take any painkillers tonight. This position. I'm sorry…'

'Roll over. It's OK. Don't stop.'

'I've broken the—'

'No. Don't talk.' She pressed her fingertips to his lips. 'It's OK. It's fine. You haven't broken anything. We'll take it easy. We'll take it differently. Easy is just as good.'

But he shook his head, eased away from her and pivoted cautiously to lie on his back. His mouth was set. In the dim light that stretched into the room from the distant kitchen, she could see him staring sightlessly and silently at the ceiling. There was nothing about his body language that encouraged her to breach the barrier he'd set up.

For a moment, she almost gave up. He was right. The mood was hopelessly broken. He'd shut her out of what he was feeling, and he didn't want her here any more. The love that burned inside her seemed like a useless emotion, incapable of softening him, incapable of getting through to him, incapable of helping him in any way. Certainly it didn't offer her any pleasure for herself at this moment.

What could she say?

Unless…

She began to stroke his chest, her fingertips slow, tantalising, light and very patient. He didn't react. Her fingers whispered across to his nipples and pinched them lightly, then she went lower, finding exquisite pleasure in the contrasts of silky skin and rougher hair, the hardness of his muscles and the careless male beauty of his nakedness.

Propping herself on one elbow, she slid her body half onto his chest. Her nipples brushed his skin, and they were so sensitised now that just this was enough to send pulses clamouring through her whole body.

'Touch me,' she whispered, and lifted his hand to place it on her breast.

For a moment, his fingers felt lifeless, uninterested. She slid a little further, one thigh brushing deliberately across his groin. He shuddered, and this time, once more, it was need. It wasn't pain.

'Touch me, Dylan,' she said again. 'Please?'

A fraction of a second later, she felt his thumb trace the peaked contour of her nipple, while his other hand came up to lift her weight. Sliding even higher, she brought her breasts within reach of his hot mouth, and at last they began to find the rhythm and urgency they'd so nearly lost. When her moving hips brought both of them crashing over the brink, she had tears spilling onto his face and onto the pillow beside him.

He must have felt them, but he didn't say anything. She lay on top of him, her head pillowed on his chest, listening to his heartbeat. It must have been ten minutes before he spoke, and his voice was creaky and stiff.

'Presumably, you have to get to work soon.'

'Yes. What's the time?'

'Clock's just there on the bedside table. I can't see it from this angle.'

'Ten past ten.'

Another silence.

'I'm first on Graham Barlow's list tomorrow,' he said.

'So, no food after midnight?'

'All that stuff. They probably would have admitted me today if I hadn't been a doctor myself. I had the pre-op check-up on Wednesday and everything was OK.'

'It won't be a long procedure, will it?'

'An hour or so, I'd guess. They'll send the tumour to Pathology. Funny, I'm not so concerned about that—the possibility that it's malignant. I'm more concerned about...'

He didn't finish, but she could guess the rest. She waited, then asked, 'When will you be discharged?'

Silence.

'Depends,' he answered at last.

Oh, dear God, of course it did! she realised. How stupid of her to have even asked! It depended on how well he could walk, how much relearning he had to do. How to get out of a chair. How to climb stairs. How to stand without falling. If his nerve damage was extensive, he might be in hospital and rehab for some time.

'You should go, Annabelle.' It didn't take half an hour to get to Coronation Hospital from his place. He meant, I want you to go. I want to be alone. Stare my future in the face, alone.

She didn't argue, just slid away from him awkwardly, aching at once for the lost contact and the lost warmth. Dylan stayed on the bed. He didn't watch her dress. All the same, she felt vulnerable as she reached for the briefs and jeans flung on the floor near the doorway, and her breasts felt swollen and sore—almost bruised. Although it was dark, and there was no one to see, she cupped her hands over them inadequately as she went in search of her bra and top in the living room.

Dylan appeared in the bedroom doorway, fully dressed, hair tousled and still faintly damp, just as she was ready to leave. He cleared his throat and opened his mouth to speak, but then he just shook his head.

'Don't be late for work,' he said finally.

Not the words she'd wanted to hear. He switched on the light, and once they'd both gone past their half-blinded reaction, she could see a potent mix of negative feelings smouldering in the depths of his eyes.

CHAPTER TEN

WHEN a patient was under general anaesthesia, he or she lost the subconscious awareness of time passing that was present in normal sleep. Dylan closed his eyes, began to count backwards from a hundred, as instructed, and woke again a millisecond later, in a bed in the recovery annexe.

Dimly, he knew that his surgery was over. His mouth felt dry, and his eyelids were too heavy to open. His lower back throbbed, and a tiny, wobbly shift in his position, lying on his side, made him aware of the dressing that covered his surgical site. A scratchy sound emerged from his lips, and one of the nurses came over. He knew her. Older woman. Pat Gould.

'Awake, Dr Calford?'

'Bit.'

'Let's check you out.' She took his temperature, blood pressure and pulse. Satisfactory, apparently—he couldn't summon the energy to ask for the exact figures—but he knew he'd be here for another half hour or so, just to make sure.

Can I move my legs?

He was sane enough not to try and answer this question yet. The effect of the anaesthesia was still weighing too heavily on his muscles. 'Barlow?' he asked Pat, just before she left.

'He's going to talk to you after his next procedure is over.'

'Tumour's out?'

'Yes, but that's all I know.'

''Anks,' was all he could manage, and even that was an effort. He closed his eyes and let the anaesthesia win for a while.

'Dylan?' said a soft voice a little later.

No, that wasn't Graham Barlow. He knew who it was.

This time, he got his eyes open. Lids felt a bit lighter now.

'I saw you just as you were getting wheeled in,' Annabelle said. 'There was no time to say anything. We were late finishing this morning, after a peritonitis case.'

'Very late off,' he said. One eye managed to focus on the clock. It was after ten.

'No.' She shook her head. 'I went home. Gave Mum and Duncan breakfast and took Mum home. Dunc's playing with a friend this morning.'

'So you should be asleep.' Tongue was working much better now.

She smiled tentatively. 'Well, I'm not. Not yet.'

Dylan's heart lurched. Lord, he was glad she was here! He was flooded with the feeling suddenly. The ripe beauty of her figure, the richness of her hair, the warmth of her smile. The familiarity of her voice and the radiance of her care.

He would have reached up a hand and touched her, squeezed her, only the hand was still too heavy. He would have said something about what was in his heart, but the only words that filled his mind had too many unanswered questions crowding around them.

Most importantly, did he have the right to say anything at all? And would she want him to? What had she wanted to give him last night, when she'd given him her body in bed? Just that? Just the immediate blessing of oblivion and release? Or much more?

Hell, it was all so woolly in his mind!

'How are you feeling?' Graham Barlow asked, coming up beside Annabelle. He gave her a quick nod, as if she was just a nurse he vaguely knew, not anyone important. Dylan rebelled inside. Annabelle was utterly important.

'Getting there,' he said. 'Tell me, Graham. Annabelle can hear it. I want her to. It's fine.'

'Nothing to tell yet,' the neurosurgeon said. 'We got it out. It's encapsulated, and almost certainly benign but, of course, Anne Smyth in Pathology will have a good look at it to make sure. You won't get the full picture on the extent of nerve damage, if any, until the whole thing has healed and you've had some physio.'

'Damage, if any,' Dylan echoed.

'I did the best possible job I could. There's a slight chance you'll experience no permanent loss of function at all. That's the best I can say.'

'OK. Thanks.' Dylan gave an awkward nod at his colleague, and tried not to let the dread and helplessness show on his face.

'We're going to send you up to the ward now, Dr Calford,' Pat Gould said a few minutes after Graham Barlow had gone.

'I'll come up with you,' Annabelle jumped in at once. She didn't care if Dylan didn't want her. She was here, and she was staying.

He still seemed very groggy, and his body, beneath the heavy white cotton of the hospital sheets, looked so different from the way it had looked last night. There was a strong chance it would never be the same body again. It was just as solid, just as strong, but so heavy and lifeless in his bed. This didn't matter to her, but she was certain that it would matter to him.

It was her own fault. She knew that, too. If she hadn't rebuffed his help, if she hadn't been so afraid of falling into the same unequal partnership that she and Alex had negotiated with each other, and if she hadn't been afraid of following Vic's emotional path as well, things might have been different now. They might have been going through this together.

Dylan had his eyes closed as they went along the corridor, up in the big service lift and into the sixth-floor neurological ward. He opened them as his bed was pushed into position in his private room, and he smiled at her. Her heart jumped and turned over in her chest. If he sent her away... Now, or *ever*.

'When do you have to go?' he asked.

'By lunchtime.' She leaned forward and stroked his shoulder tentatively, ending at the ropy hardness of his forearm.

He twisted his arm a little beneath her touch, and suddenly her fingers were engulfed in his grip. He closed his eyes again, and she just sat there, his touch bringing back powerful images of last night, and the way they'd made love with such urgent intensity.

Was that only because it had been their last chance?

'What are we going to do, Annabelle?' he asked in a scratchy voice.

'Whatever you want.'

Dylan laughed without moving his mouth, eyes still closed. His face looked just as gorgeous and dear to her when it was still and slack as it did when firmed and animated by his work in surgery...or his energy in the pool...or when he kissed her.

'What I want isn't good enough,' he said. 'My career may be over. I may be half-crippled.'

'All right, then we'll do what *I* want,' Annabelle said.

'And what's that?'

'We'll stop this stupid, almost *competitive* game we've both been playing since Alex walked out of the wedding. This game of tallying up which of us needs the other the most, and which of us has the most to give. We've both handled it wrongly. Maybe there was no way to stop that from happening at first, but if we don't change it now...' She stopped.

If we don't change it now, how will we make our love work?

That was what she'd wanted to say, but she still didn't know if he loved her at all, let alone if he was thinking of a long-term future to what he felt. *She* was.

Annabelle watched his face, and saw him nod faintly. Had he understood?

He still had his eyes shut, and his lips were closed and joined by a soft seam. She wanted to kiss them open, and feel his fingers tangling in her hair, the way they had tangled there last night. More than that, she wanted to hear what he would say.

She waited, but nothing came.

'Gone to sleep again?' said one of the ward nurses, a minute later.

Oh, heavens, he had! she realised. Of course he had! He was less than two hours post-op, he was on medication for pain, and sleep would be the best place in the world for him. How could she even have tried to talk to him now?

'I'll come back later,' Annabelle said.

But would he want her when she did?

'Can you drop by on your way to work, Annabelle?'

Dylan was on the phone from his hospital bed, sounding so much stronger and more alert than he had ten hours ago. He sounded a little grim, too, as if phoning her was something he had needed to do—an unpleasant duty—not something he wanted. 'We didn't get a chance to finish our conversation this morning,' he finished.

'No, we didn't,' she agreed. 'So you do remember it, then?'

'No, not exactly,' he admitted. 'But I know it was important.'

'I'll—I'll give you a recap or something.' She could hardly speak.

'So you'll come?'

'Yes, I'll leave here as soon as I can.'

Duncan wasn't in bed yet, but he soon would be. Annabelle didn't know what to think about Dylan's call. Did he want to talk about last night?

Thanks, he might say. It took my mind off things. But don't get the wrong idea.

Or perhaps there was some news about the extent of damage to his nerves.

When she arrived at the hospital forty minutes later, Dylan was sitting up in bed. He looked tired and a little creased, but it suited him…made her want to smooth out those lines around his eyes and mouth with her fingers, and with her lips… And there was life in his face again.

He had his wheeled meal tray beside him, with an open paperback novel sitting on it, as well as a pile of chocolate boxes, and his raised knees had turned the sheet into a tent. Surrounding him, the entire private room was ablaze with flowers.

There were red roses and exotic tropical blooms in yellow and purple and white. There were lilies and carnations and daisies, and *more* roses—pink ones, gold ones, furled buds and open blooms. There were flowers in pots and flowers in Cellophane, and flowers bunched with gold ribbon, and the only thing that could possibly compete with the flowers for her attention were the chocolates…and Dylan.

Annabelle spoke her first thought aloud. 'You've phoned your family!' Surely all these flowers and gifts had to be from them. 'Oh, I'm so glad! Are they coming out?'

He shook his head. 'I haven't phoned them yet. I told you I wanted to wait. These yellow ones are from Alex. You left this box of chocolates, according to the card…'

'Yes, this morning. I went out and came back with them, but you were still asleep.'

'But the rest of the chocolates and the flowers are for you.'

'For…?' It didn't make sense. They were overwhelming, lush and perfect, lavish and expensive and decadent and sweet. They brought tears to her eyes. He really wasn't well enough to have spent half the afternoon on the phone, ordering chocolates and flowers. For *her*.

'From me,' he said softly. 'For everything.'

'Dylan!'

'For *everything*,' he repeated. 'I couldn't wait any

longer to say it, and prove it, and what could I do in this bed all afternoon but order chocolates and flowers? For the way I love you, for the way you gave yourself to me last night, without knowing what was going on between us, and when I was so apprehensive I could hardly see straight. For the words I want to say to you now, which I'm still afraid you'll throw back in my face. I've been a brute to you this past week, not trusting why you were still around.'

'I know why I was still around,' she said softly, sliding onto the bed to sit close to him.

'And I hope I do, too, now. I love you, Annabelle. Marry me!' He took her hands, and warmth flooded up her arms.

'Oh, Dylan!'

'I wanted to wait until I knew…about my legs. The tumour is benign. Graham got the report back late this afternoon. So at least I can promise you my life.'

Dylan's life was more than enough. Annabelle wanted to say it, but her heart was so full she couldn't find the words and, anyway, he didn't give her time.

'But because of the rest—my career, and the question of me being able to walk properly, I was going to wait,' he said. 'Then, though… I think you said something this morning. What was it?'

'You fell asleep!' Annabelle's tears welled again, threatening to brim over.

'I'm very awake now, and I remember it all. It doesn't matter which of us takes and which of us gives. That'll balance out. We can't keep score. It's deathly to do that, in any relationship. I love you, and I'm going to trust that that's enough. Enough for both of us.'

'Oh, it is. I love you, and it *is*. Whatever happens. It's more than enough.'

'No matter which of us has to do the most giving? And what form that giving takes?'

'Yes. No matter. It's not important. I'll marry you, Dylan, as soon as you want.'

He reached up and touched her face, and she bent towards him. Their lips met, and their kiss sealed the moment for both of them—the perfect promise of forever.

'Put me down, Gwanpa!' Duncan protested loudly.

Distracted, Dylan and Annabelle both looked at the little boy, struggling in Dylan's father's arms.

'All right, little guy,' said Mason Calford, in his deep-voiced American accent. 'We'll go for a walk, OK?'

Annabelle watched for another few seconds, to make sure the older man and the little boy were genuinely happy in each other's company, then turned back to her groom. The guests, gathered in the informal garden setting of one of Brisbane's most beautiful public parks, fell silent. The marriage celebrant cleared his throat then apologised and searched in his pocket for a handkerchief. Linda, Annabelle's newly pregnant bridesmaid, gave a nervous hiccup. The best man, Dylan's close friend David, shifted his feet.

'I've just thought of something,' Dylan said quietly in Annabelle's ear. 'We were supposed to get back to the celebrant if we wanted any changes in the standard format of the ceremony, and we never did.'

'You mean the lines about—?'

'Yes. If anyone knows any reason why this couple should not be joined, and so on.'

'Pretty significant lines, those can be. Are you worried?' She smiled at him, and caught his answering grin.

He wore a dark suit which emphasised his broad shoulders, and he was very steady on his feet. It was over three months since his surgery now. The first week had been difficult, as the surgical site had slowly healed. For several days, they had all been afraid that his effortful, hesitant and ungainly walking and standing would be permanent.

Time, however, had proved otherwise. Dylan had worked hard and consistently at his physiotherapy, and there was only a minor numbness remaining in his toes—not enough to compromise his performance during surgery or change his normal gait.

Their June wedding, with his family in attendance from America and the sun shining mild and bright in the afternoon sky, was almost as much a celebration of his health as it was a celebration of their soon-to-be-joined lives.

Almost as much. They were both determined that their marriage would always come first in their shared priorities. They wanted children of their own, in the not-too-distant future, and they both agreed that Annabelle should put her career on hold for the time being. Duncan and Mum both needed her too much. She expected that the coming years would be both full and rich.

'No, I'm not worried at all,' Annabelle answered her groom. 'You can object all you like, and so can anyone else. But *this* time, come hell or high water, Dylan Calford, the wedding is going ahead!'

'You won't get any arguments from me, my darling,' he whispered, and they both joined hands as the celebrant began his opening words.

Modern Romance™
...seduction and
passion guaranteed

Tender Romance™
...love affairs that
last a lifetime

Medical Romance™
...medical drama
on the pulse

Historical Romance™
...rich, vivid and
passionate

Sensual Romance™
...sassy, sexy and
seductive

Blaze Romance™
...the temperature's
rising

27 new titles every month.

Live the emotion

MILLS & BOON®

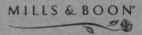

MILLS & BOON®

Medical Romance™

DAISY AND THE DOCTOR by *Meredith Webber*

Dr Julian Austin doesn't believe in love – so psychologist Daisy is his perfect bride. She's been hurt too often to trust in love. Then Daisy realises that, for her, marriage to Julian would be exactly the love match she wants to avoid – and Julian starts to wonder – if love doesn't exist, what's happening to his heart?

THE SURGEON'S MARRIAGE by *Maggie Kingsley*

Doctors Tom and Helen Brooke have a great marriage – when they can find time to see each other. Despite being overworked and under-appreciated, Helen knows she and Tom have something special. Then a series of misunderstandings makes her think that Tom doesn't care – and Tom is faced with a fight to save his marriage…

THE MIDWIFE'S BABY WISH by *Gill Sanderson*

As Keldale's midwife, Lyn Pierce is kept busy! But when Dr Adam Fletcher joins the practice he awakens emotions she can't afford to let herself feel. For it soon becomes clear that Adam wants a family – and while Lyn can give him love, giving him the children he longs for is an impossible dream…

On sale 4th April 2003

Available at most branches of WH Smith, Tesco, Martins, Borders, Eason, Sainsbury's and all good paperback bookshops.

0303/03a

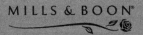

MILLS & BOON®

Medical Romance™

DR DALLORI'S BRIDE by *Carol Wood*

For the last six months Dr Antonio Dallori has tried
to forget Laura Bright. He met her only once, and
was intrigued by their encounter. So he's elated when
Laura returns to the village as his new practice nurse!
Laura is incredibly attracted to Antonio – but she has
a baby to think of now...

DELIVERING SECRETS by *Fiona McArthur*

Midwife Ellie Diamond convinces herself that it is the
chance to bring up her son in an idyllic coastal town
that has lured her back to Bell's River. It has nothing
to do with the chance to work with her former love,
obstetrician Dr Luke Farrell – the man Ellie promised
to return to five years ago...

HIS EMERGENCY FIANCÉE by *Kate Hardy*

Playboy A&E doctor Ben Robertson needs a fiancée –
quick! He invented one to keep a certain person
happy – and now she is demanding to meet his bride-
to-be! Ben has no choice but to beg his housemate,
surgeon Kirsty Brown, to play the part. Kirsty agrees
– reluctantly. So why is she suddenly wishing she was
his real fiancée after all?

On sale 4th April 2003

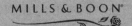

FREE

2 BOOKS
AND A SURPRISE GIFT!

We would like to take this opportunity to thank you for reading this Mills & Boon® book by offering you the chance to take TWO more specially selected titles from the Medical Romance™ series absolutely FREE! We're also making this offer to introduce you to the benefits of the Reader Service™—

- ★ FREE home delivery
- ★ FREE monthly Newsletter
- ★ FREE gifts and competitions
- ★ Exclusive Reader Service discount
- ★ Books available before they're in the shops

Accepting these FREE books and gift places you under no obligation to buy; you may cancel at any time, even after receiving your free shipment. Simply complete your details below and return the entire page to the address below. **You don't even need a stamp!**

YES! Please send me 2 free Medical Romance books and a surprise gift. I understand that unless you hear from me, I will receive 4 superb new titles every month for just £2.60 each, postage and packing free. I am under no obligation to purchase any books and may cancel my subscription at any time. The free books and gift will be mine to keep in any case.

M3ZEC

Ms/Mrs/Miss/Mr ....Initials ....

BLOCK CAPITALS PLEASE

Surname ....

Address ....

....

....Postcode ....

Send this whole page to:
UK: FREEPOST CN81, Croydon, CR9 3WZ
EIRE: PO Box 4546, Kilcock, County Kildare (stamp required)

Offer valid in UK and Eire only and not available to current Reader Service subscribers to this series. We reserve the right to refuse an application and applicants must be aged 18 years or over. Only one application per household. Terms and prices subject to change without notice. Offer expires 30th June 2003. As a result of this application, you may receive offers from Harlequin Mills & Boon and other carefully selected companies. If you would prefer not to share in this opportunity please write to The Data Manager at the address above.

Mills & Boon® is a registered trademark owned by Harlequin Mills & Boon Limited.
Medical Romance™ is being used as a trademark.